To Nikki

Into The Deep

T.a. McKay

Follow your heart...
Into The Deep

TMcKay

2

Into The Deep

Trademark acknowledgements:

The author acknowledges the trademarked status and trademark owners of the following trademarks mentioned in this work of fiction:

Subaru: Fuji Heavy Industries (FHI)

Lexus: Toyota (GB) PLC (Lexus Division)

Dirty Dancer by Enrique Iglesias with Usher featuring Little Wayne:

Writers~ Enrique Iglesias, Nadir Khayat, Evan Bogart, Erika Nuri, David Quinones.

Producer~ RedOne

Label ~ Universal Republic, Universal Latino

Dedication

To my husband, Stuart.

You pushed me at every point during this process even though I was an absent wife and mother. You picked up the slack without complaining...too much!

Thank you for always believing in me.

To my kids ~ Brandon, Xander and Rhianna.

Thank you for understanding that mum lost her mind for a little bit. Yes there were a lot of pyjama days, and days where your dinner was late but you always had a hug for me when I got behind on things.

To my mum, Lorraine.

You always taught me that I needed to follow my dreams. Well I did it! Even if this book isn't successful I did it! I have a book with my name on it. Thank you for teaching me never to give up.

I love you all more than words can ever say. You all give me the strength I need and the love that keeps me moving forward.

To the moon and back!

Prologue

And I think I may have just lost my hearing. No, that's not right. I can still hear him droning on about something and I'm pretty sure he's trying to tell me something important. Maybe it's just a dream. Or should that be a nightmare? That's what it is. I'm asleep, and I just need to wake myself up. Yes, a dream. That's why my vision can't focus, and I'm having difficulty breathing, or it's maybe a panic attack? That would make sense because it feels like something heavy is pressing down hard on my chest.

"Makenzie, are you ok? I know it's a shock, but these things happen." I look at Carl with his perfect blonde hair and he looks so calm, and suddenly I want to attack him...or push him out the window...or attack him and *then* push him out of the window.

"These things happen? These things happen? How the fuck can you say that these things just happen?" I scream at him finally losing my cool as the reality of what he has just said to me sinks in. How can he stand there and make it seem as though like I'm the one overreacting to this?

"I really don't think there is any need for that kind of language Makenzie. We're all adults here, and I'm sure we can act like it." *Is. He. Kidding?* He's standing there right in front of me looking as though he has just informed me it's raining outside. Does he not understand that my life has just changed forever?

"Please tell me that you're not trying to make me feel bad for swearing, when you have just admitted to me that you are fucking your PA! If that wasn't bad enough, you've got her pregnant, and now you're leaving me so you can go and play

7

happy families together!" Oh, this feels good. Screaming at him so everyone around us knows that he can't keep it in his pants during company time feels amazing. I need to keep my anger going, or I am going to crumble. A bit like my entire life at the moment, but I refuse to give him the satisfaction of witnessing my pain. Taking a deep breath I move forward and towards where they're both standing. He's standing right beside her! At least he has the decency to look embarrassed, though I wish that I knew for certain whether it's from what he's putting me through or is it because everyone was looking at the three of us through his open office door. I'm standing on one side of his desk with my hands firmly placed on the top to keep myself upright, Carl ever the gentleman, is standing on the other side of the desk and is slightly in front of Rose with his arm protectively out to the side and over her belly. I don't know if it's to keep me from her or to keep her quiet. I just think it's wrong to see him standing with her. Rose the now obvious reason that Carl has been working so late recently. Rose who has been sleeping with my fiancé, while I have been waiting at home for him to finish work so I can cook for him. Rose the bitch with her paid for blonde hair and her bought perky boobs and her perfect size 10 body. Rose who is now carrying my fiancé's baby and holding his hand at this moment and I really want to slap the cocky smile off her face! I'm not a violent person, but I think I'm justified on this occasion to want to do harm to both of them, just a little and hopefully permanently.

"Makenzie, I'm sorry. I never meant for any of this to happen, I really didn't, but I can't change anything about that now. We're having a baby, and you know I have always wanted a family." He pleads with me gently.

"Yes, but I thought you meant with me." This time I can't control the tear that escapes my eye and rolls down my cheek. I wipe it away angrily with the back of my hand and look him in the eye. Those beautiful green eyes that I have spent the last three years looking into while we laughed together, and cried together and made love together.

"Sweetheart, you know I love you, but I can't turn my back on Rose now that she's pregnant." Rose turns her head so quickly to look at him that pieces of her perfectly styled blonde hair falls across her face, she moves it out of the way while she scowls at Carl. I would feel sorry for her, and what she is hearing, I mean he has basically just admitted that he is with her just for the baby, but I just can't bring myself to feel bad. As my mother always told me when I was growing up, she has made her bed and now she will have to lie in it.

"Were you thinking about how much you loved me when this started? I mean, I thought we were going to spend the rest of our lives together. We have booked our wedding, our honeymoon. You must have been sleeping with her when we were organising things. I have my dress ordered, and we have booked the country house to get married in. How can you do this to me? I don't understand? Was I not enough? Did I do something wrong?" I know I'm rambling, but I just can't seem to stop myself now that I've started. I need answers from him, but instead he is just standing there looking at me with pain in his eyes. He doesn't get to be the one in pain here, he caused all this, and this is all on him! He walks around the desk and pulls me into his strong arms, he feels so good holding me, protecting me from the pain. If I could just stay here forever everything will be ok, nothing can hurt while he is holding me.

"I'm sorry I'm putting you through this, if I could go back and change it I would." He whispers in my ear as tears start to fall without control down my cheeks.

9

"Carl! What exactly are you saying here?" Her voice pulls me back to reality, I push against his chest until he lets me go, I look up into his sad eyes and I do the only thing I can think to do...I slap him!

Chapter one

"Damn!" I mutter quietly to myself into the night. *I'm such a klutz.* I'm pretty sure that I'm the only person in the whole damn world who could spill coffee all over themselves just sitting on a park bench. I place the cup down to the side of me on the bench and go to pull my t-shirt away from my skin. I pull the neck of my t-shirt away from my body and blow downwards, the coffee is scalding hot, and I'm hoping it doesn't leave a red mark on my skin. Why this morning? All I wanted was to sit quietly in the park and take some time to collect my thoughts. Why is everything so goddamn hard these days? What could I have possibly done in a past life to make Karma want to kick my ass now? Ever since Carl had left me, my world has crumbled before my very eyes. Well, saying that he left is technically a lie. I'm the one who left him, but only after he made my life implode in on itself. I don't think that my luck can get any worse at the moment. I've lost my fiancé. My house. I've even lost my job. I know I really shouldn't complain because the company did offer me a promotion. They said I would get all my moving expenses paid for me, including my accommodation, and other company benefits.

I think they were worried that I'd make a huge fuss if I stayed in my office with Carl. Of course having daddy as one of the main shareholders means that he got to keep his current position in the business, and someone had to leave.

There was only one downside to the new job they offered me. To take the position, it would mean I would have to move across the Atlantic and settle in New York. I have to admit, I was extremely tempted to take them up on the offer. A fresh start in a new country could have been just what I needed, but after thinking about it long and hard I decided that I couldn't just up and leave my family behind in the UK. Even though when I think about it, losing my family doesn't feel like it would be such a big loss at the moment. As much as I love them they still seem to think that I should have fought harder to hold onto Carl, even after everything he put me through. My parents were highly embarrassed by the whole situation and wanted to act like it never happened. Well at least that's one thing we have in common, I wish that it had never happened either.

I sit and brood over my thoughts as I look out over the park. It's early. So early, in fact, that the sun hasn't even started to rise yet. It's this time of day that I have started to love the most. It's so peaceful because most people are still in their beds, which is where I should be, but I don't seem too able to sleep much these days.

The air is already beginning to get warm, and I know by lunch it's going to be another scorcher. Fantastic! It has been unseasonably hot the last few weeks and being the typical Brit that I am, I pray for hot weather. That is until we actually get some. My apartment has been like a pressure cooker even with the windows opened up fully, with not as much as a breeze blowing through the air. I'm just beginning to settle down again with my coffee and a new list of things to stress about entering my mind, when I hear a noise from behind me. Before I even have the time to react, I hear a deep voice.

"Are you all right?"

I let out a squeal and jump up from the bench. I turn and quickly prepare my flight or fight response. I hadn't taken all of those self-defence classes for nothing. By the time I've turned half circle to face him I've dropped my coffee to the ground and braced myself to attack. What I see is actually a little funny. The guy is standing with his hands out in front of him and appears to be in a calming stance.

"I'm sorry...I'm really, really sorry. I didn't mean to startle you."

I relax a little and will my racing heart rate to slow because with my luck recently, I'll end up having a heart attack or something. I keep my eyes trained on him and take him in. He's really tall, maybe about 6ft 2, but then everyone and everything seems really tall compared to my 5ft 3inch height. He has dark hair, though I can't quite tell the true colour because of the lack of lighting. It's hard to make out his face in the shadows, but I am able to make out his build. He's lean yet muscly, all at the same time. He has arms that look strong, especially where his muscles are bulging against the sleeves of his workout top. His shoulders are huge, and I'm pretty sure that if I were to even try and fight him off, I would fail very quickly.

What surprises me the most though is his thin waist. I can see that he has muscle there, but compared to his arms it's just not what you would expect to see, that's all.

He's wearing knee length black shorts, accompanied with a black workout top. It looks like a second skin, and let me tell you, if the sight in front of me is anything to go by, the first skin looks as though it could be absolutely glorious. I relax a little bit more. He isn't exactly dressed like he's out and about to attack some random person.

He has a backpack slung casually over his shoulder, and he's wearing extremely smart trainers on his feet. I'm beginning to wonder where he's going because he looks as though he's dressed and ready to hit the gym, though there isn't one around here for miles. Then I wonder why on earth I'm standing here and checking out some guy when he could be anyone. This isn't the safest of places or situations to be in, especially in the company of a complete stranger. But for some reason, I can't seem to take my eyes off of him.

"Are you ok?" he asks again, his voice taking me out of the little dream world I've found myself in.

"Eh ... yes. Thanks. I'm fine." I manage, lowering my hands as my gaze drops down to look longingly at the remnants of my coffee.

"I heard you shouting and I wanted to make sure everything was okay. You know, you really shouldn't be out in the park at this time on your own. It's not safe." Wow, he has a great voice. Soft, velvety and very deep. You know those voices you hear on the television, and they can sell you anything ... *twice*?

"Oh yeah, I'm fine. I spilt my coffee, and it burned a little. I didn't realise I'd been so loud. And there's really no need to worry. I come out here at this time a lot, and you're actually the first person I've seen."

Why did I just offer that piece of information to him? Talk about inviting trouble, I don't know him from the next guy and now he knows I'm here regularly on my own, with no one within earshot to hear my screams.

"Really? I pass here every morning and I haven't seen you before."

"Yeah, well you see, I don't usually spill my coffee all over myself. I'm usually pretty quiet." I say with a smile. The returning smile I receive from him has me almost having to catch my breath. His smile matches his dreamy voice, and although I could easily stand here all day with him, I'm beginning to feel a little awkward as we continue to stand and stare at one another, with complete silence taking over the space between us.

"Well, thanks for checking that everything's okay. Don't let me hold you up any longer." I say and turn to pick up the now empty cup. As I walk over to put it in the bin next to the bench, he speaks again.

"Well as long as you're sure you're okay then I'll get going. It was nice to meet you." He begins to walk in the opposite direction than where I'm heading and when I'm only a few steps down the pathway, I hear him shout.

"Hey, beautiful! My name's Rocco by the way!"

I turn back and see him smiling in my direction as he continues to walk backwards down the path.

"I'm Makenzie." I shout back.

What harm could it possibly do?

****

I'm sitting at a small table in my kitchen, and I've been trying to update my CV on my laptop, but I'm failing miserably. It's far too hot in here, and there's no relief to be had, even with the window next to me opened up wide. I really wish this place had air conditioning. I begin to wonder how long you can go without food before you starve, because, at this moment, I'm considering foregoing all of next week's meals so I can get it fitted.

My thoughts also keep drifting back to a certain hot guy named Rocco, which doesn't seem to be helping my body temperature go down any. The sound of his voice and the outline of his amazing body is actually really hard to try and forget. I realise though that thinking about him is wasting time that I don't have. I need to find a job and fast. My savings aren't going to last me forever, and I don't relish the idea of ending up homeless.

I moved into this place after Carl and I split up. I lost a lot when we parted ways. We'd lived together in a beautiful townhouse in the heart of London. The house was in his name only, so I wasn't entitled to anything, even though I'd helped him pay for it the whole time we were together. Now, here I am, living in a one bedroomed apartment, above a shoe shop in a small town that's located just outside of Southampton. It's clean, cheap, and it's quiet, so I can't really ask for much more. No, that's a lie. If I could have one more thing, it would be my old house back. The one with the big garden and the dressing room and the huge Victorian bathtub. Having none of these now just depresses me more. I miss my bath the most. Having to live with just a shower room isn't something that I particularly enjoy. I miss wasting my Sunday afternoons away in the bath with a glass of white wine and my kindle. I still don't understand why I had to lose so much while he was able to walk away with everything. He was the one who made a mess of everything, not me. That should have been my life, and he and that bitch took it all away from me.

Turning to looking at the ever-growing pile of bills, I inwardly groan, I don't even know where to start being able to catch up with them. Turning back to stare at my CV on the computer screen, I hope to find a little inspiration for what I need to do next. I open another window on my computer and begin to search for any local jobs that are currently being advertised, there must be something that would suit me. I don't drive, so the job must be as local as possible, and it has to be accessible on foot or by bus. This definitely limits what I can take by a large margin.

As I'm scrolling down through the adverts, I notice a vacancy for a receptionist at the local swimming pool. I wasn't even aware that we had a swimming pool around here. Granted, I haven't long since moved to the area, but you'd think that I would have noticed it.

I open up the advert and see that it's just on the other side of the park. Now I feel really dumb for missing it, I make a promise to myself that I'll make an extra effort to get out and explore the local area more. The fact that it is so close to where I live is the reason I fill in the attached application form. I'm not the biggest fan of swimming pools, in fact, if I'm to be completely honest, I have a paralysing fear of them, but if the job is restricted to the reception area only though, I think it should be fine.

I know that it's not exactly a job in publishing, but I'm pretty sure my bills don't care what I do as long as I can manage to pay them. As I press the send key, I whisper a small prayer and cross my fingers. I'm pretty sure that if I had a lucky rabbit's foot on hand, I'd be rubbing it right now too. I *need* a job. After continuing to search the webpage for more vacancies for a while I decide that I have done enough searching for the day, there's nothing else that would be suitable. Most of them are too far away to be accessible, and the others are, well, let's just say that I'm not at the stage where I need to clean windows just yet. I switch the computer off and spin in my chair as I look around my tiny apartment. I need something to keep myself entertained, and in the process, hopefully something that'll help to cool me down. Making a mental list in my mind of all the things that I have the energy to do, I find that I'm left with only one option. A shower it is then.

After taking my second cool shower of the day, I tie my hair back and go to grab my Kindle. I want to finish the great book I'm currently reading. Today is definitely not a day to be venturing outside. The heat that's beaming down from the sun is making it far too uncomfortable to make the outdoors enjoyable.

I pass by my computer, and the flashing email icon catches my eye. It's most likely to be spam, but I decide to open it anyway. I don't have anything else planned for the rest of the day and so this might help to take up a few minutes.

After reading it for a few seconds, I let out a small chuckle, one of almost relief. I've actually been offered an interview for the job at the pool. I feel myself becoming a little panicked when I see that they have asked if I can be there in a few hours, but I decide to take this as a good sign.

I send them a quick reply, telling them that I'll be there, before racing through to my bedroom so I can dress in something a little more professional. Or, at least something that isn't jean shorts and a tank top. I don't have any idea on what to wear. I need something that will keep me cool as I walk there though, I don't think that turning up a sweaty mess will make a great first impression.

Once I've decided on a black gypsy skirt, which reaches down to my ankles, a light white summer top and some strappy sandals, I leave my apartment and make my way across the park so I can try and locate the pool. I turn and glance at the bench I usually take up residence on as I walk past. The whole place really does look different in the daylight. Unfortunately though, looking at the bench also makes me picture Rocco, with his perfect body and swoon worthy voice.

Stop! I tell myself quietly. I need to forget about him. I only met him for five minutes. We had one conversation. I need to get my brain to listen to me for once. It always goes back to that brief meeting. Leaving the park. I turn to the left and there it is, right in front of me. How the hell did I manage to miss this place? It's an enormous building and is located approximately one hundred yards along the pathway. The front wall is made up of tinted glass windows and the sign outside states 'Clear Water Pool'. Everything that I can see from the outside doesn't help with my excuses for not noticing it before now. Entering the building, I'm met with a cool blast of air from their amazing air conditioning unit, and at this point I've decided that I really want this job.

Leaving with what feels like the first smile in a long time, I decide that perhaps my luck is beginning to change. I got the job! I know it's probably because they're desperate for help, but I don't care. I'm still over the moon that it was me who got it.

When I first arrived at the reception desk, the poor manager was running around and seemed highly harassed. He'd been trying to cover the front desk, the telephones, and the deliveries that were arriving. I felt sorry for the slightly red faced, sweaty man and so I went behind the desk and started to answer the phone. I had absolutely no idea what I was doing, but I thought it'd be better for people to hear a voice than just continuous ringing on the other end of the line. Once it had calmed down a little, the owner, Matt, shook my hand and offered me the job on the spot. Though there was one condition. I was only able to have the job if I promised to start tomorrow.

I have an early start in the morning, so I decide to head straight home to get myself organised. I've been given a uniform, so at least I don't have to worry about what to wear. Walking home, I don't really notice the heat as much as I did earlier, so I take my time and walk leisurely through the park. It may be a while before I can enjoy the daytime chaos of the children and dogs running around again. I smile as I slowly make my way towards my apartment. Yeah, things certainly seem to be looking up.

Chapter Two

Wow, I'm really not used to being up so early. Why is it that when you need to get up for something you never want to? I hit the snooze button on my alarm clock twice before I can muster up enough energy to crawl out of bed. But here I am, ready to leave, and it's only 4.45am.

I'm showered, dressed and I've already consumed two cups of coffee while trying to wake myself up properly before I head out. I just need to keep reminding myself that if I start early, then I finish early, and I think I'm going to need something to keep me going in a few hours' time. I have a feeling that the next eight hours might be the longest if my life. The uniform I'm wearing consists of black knee length capri pants, an electric blue fitted t-shirt and comfortable black trainers. They look good together, and I'm sure they're going to be comfortable to work in.

I check myself in the mirror and realise that I don't look quite as bad as I'd been expecting to at this time of the morning. I've pulled my long brown hair back into a ponytail, so it doesn't get in my way, and I've kept my makeup to a minimum, having applied only mascara and a little lip gloss.

I walk through to the kitchen and fill my travel mug with my favourite caramel flavoured mocha, before heading out the door to start my first day back in the workforce.

It's still dark outside as I make my journey to work. To think that only twenty four hours ago I was sitting on the bench, thinking about how crap my life was and how nothing was going right for me and now, a day later, I have a job that I'm hoping to enjoy. Even if I don't happen to enjoy it, at least I'll now have some money coming in.

I arrive outside the building just before I'm meant to start my shift. Upon walking inside, the smell of chlorine assaults my senses. I didn't notice how strong it was yesterday, but I put this down to the air conditioning systems. I take a deep breath as I walk further inside. If I'm going to keep this job then I'll need to overcome the memories that are associated with this very smell. It's time to start dealing with them.

I find Matt behind the reception desk, wearing a huge smile. He looks a lot more relaxed than he did yesterday, and he's obviously eager to get my training underway. I really don't think that he is much of a people person, but I think that he's sweet all the same. He's an older man and has permanent rosy cheeks. They make him look a bit like Santa.

I place my bag in the lockable drawer under the desk and for the next half hour, Matt runs through my list of procedures and duties. I'm glad that my daily routine won't take me near the pool side area. The closest I'll need to be is when I'll be in the spectator's area. Looking through the glass is perfectly fine with me.

From the way he's explaining things, I'm pretty sure that he doesn't actually have much more knowledge himself. Every couple of minutes he keeps referring back to the procedures book that the last receptionist left behind for him.

After a while, I told him that I would be fine, and if I were to have any problems or concerns, then he would be the first person I'd call. He seemed happy enough with that so right now I'm sitting in front of the computer and trying to get my head around the booking system while the place is still quiet.

I'd asked Matt why he opened the place up so early when there doesn't seem to be anyone around, though he told me that the swimming team are already in the pool and have been for a while now. Swimming team? There's another thing to add to my ever-growing knowledge of the local area. The booking system seems quite easy to use. Also on the computer is the running system for the pool and steam room area. That looks a lot more complicated than the booking system, and if I had my way, I wouldn't touch it...*ever*. But, unfortunately, that is also a part of my job. I need to monitor and check the areas, making sure that everything runs smoothly. I'm pretty sure that at some point that I'll manage to empty the pool or make the steam room ice over or something.

I continue to work through my list of observations, taking notes down in the logbook of all the readings that the computer is showing on the screen. I click into one of the sections marked 'alarm', and note that it's set at running. According to my procedures, this is correct.

As I'm clicking out of the programme, I press the wrong button. My heart stops beating in my chest as an alarm starts to sound throughout the pool.

I'm frozen in my chair, just staring at the screen. I have no idea what I need to do. We're not talking about a quiet alarm here. We're talking about an alarm that you'll be able to hear halfway down the street and one that will have everyone racing out of the pool within seconds! I start pressing everything on the screen, trying to turn it off. *Why won't it just switch off?*

"Please, please, please, please," I repeat over and over again as I hear the doors of the changing rooms opening up as the men begin to exit ... *in only towels and swimming trunks.*

"Please, please, please, please!" I continue my mantra because I'm still having a hard time working out how to turn the bloody thing off.

"Miss? You really need to leave."

I freeze right in the middle of my panicked button pressing when I hear the voice. Oh no. Please. *Please don't let it be him!* When look up, I come face to face with the very man who has consumed most of my thoughts over the past twenty-four hours. I don't think that I would have recognised him if I'd have seen him in the pool, but there's no mistaking the voice. I would recognise it anywhere, even after only our first brief encounter.

"Evacuating the whole pool, and with my mistake, losing my job on my first day," I snap. I didn't mean to, but I'm now really starting to sweat as more people make their way out onto the street whilst half naked. Thankfully, it's a warm morning.

"May I?" He asks as he moves around the desk to stand beside me. I move my chair back to give him some room. My mind isn't working with me just now. I know that in this situation and with everything that's going on I shouldn't notice, but I do. He's standing right next to me, wearing nothing but swimming trunks, and he's close enough to me that if I turn just slightly in my chair, I'd be able to lick the drops of water off his amazing abs.

I really need to get my thoughts in check because I have absolutely no idea where that even came from. I find that I'm unable to look away though. He's incredible, his skin is glistening, and the muscles of his abdomen are tightening and relaxing as he bends over to work on the computer. I have an overwhelming need to reach my hand out and touch him. I wonder if he's as solid as he appears to be. I'm pulled away from my thoughts when all of a sudden the alarm stops and silence takes over again. I look back up to his face quickly, but not before he has obviously already noticed where I was looking. When my eyes reach his face, I'm greeted with a small smile that's pulling up at the sides of his mouth.

"How did you know how to do that?" I ask trying my hardest to take his attention away from the very obvious blush I feel traveling over my face. My cheeks are burning. I can't believe that he's just caught me checking him out.

"Matt managed to do the same thing in his first week covering the job. I helped him sort it out, and I made sure to remember how to fix it. I knew there was a good chance he'd do it again."

"Well, thankfully you did because I had no idea what to do. Now I just have to get everyone back inside and apologise, and then hope that I can convince Matt not to fire me." I'm not feeling very positive on that particular thought. I turn sharply and face him when I hear him beginning to laugh. He's thrown his head right back and is laughing as though I've just told him the funniest joke in the world.

"Well, I'm glad that I could make you laugh. I didn't realise that me losing my job would be so amusing for you." I throw at him as I storm away. I need to let everyone know that they can return to the pool and changing rooms. He grabs my arm gently, turning me towards him. He takes hold of a piece of my hair that's escaped from my ponytail and places it softly behind my ear. It takes everything in my power not to melt from his touch.

"Hey, I wasn't laughing at you losing your job. I was laughing at the thought of Matt firing you for something that he's done himself." His hand feels cool from standing in the air-conditioned area with very little clothing on, but all I can feel is the heat that's beginning to spread through my arm from where he's still touching me. I look into his eyes and then realise that he's being so nice to me, but I'm being a bitch. I shouldn't be snapping at him like that, especially when he's just me helped me with the alarm.

"I'm sorry. I didn't mean to snap at you, I just really need this job and I don't want to lose it."

"You'll be fine. Listen, let's just get all these people back inside before they freeze." He says this with a smile over his lips. I try to resist, but I can't seem to stop myself from smiling widely back at him while nodding a yes.

We manage to get everyone back into the pool and changing area without too much trouble, and there are a lot of apologies made.

I sit down heavily on the chair behind my desk and let out a deep sigh. I really can't believe everything that's happened, especially in my first few hours of working here, but on the upside, I doubt that it can get any worse.

I have a little giggle to myself as I turn back to the computer and exit the damn programme, making sure that I click on the correct button this time. I finally manage to get into a flow while I continue to work through my to-do list and answer phones. I'm learning a lot from the people on the phones about what we actually offer. There's a small gym, steam room, a sports massage therapist that comes in four times a week, and then obviously the pool itself. Not just that, it also has numerous conference rooms that can be booked for parties or meetings. I have to keep asking myself again, how the hell did I miss this place? I'm totally engrossed in my work when Matt walks up behind me and taps me lightly on the shoulder. I just about jump out of my skin. Why am I so jumpy these days?

"Good afternoon, Makenzie. How are things going?"

I glance up at him and wonder how much I should tell him about the day so far. I would accidentally on purpose forget to mention the whole alarm thing, but the fact that he'll talk to the people that were evacuated this morning, I know I have to break it to him first.

"Em … yeah it's ... eh, good," I stutter. 'Come on girl! *Grow a pair and tell him'*, I scold myself in my head.

"There was a slight mishap earlier, but I got everything back under control and everyone seemed happy when they left." I know they had been because they were all laughing at me when they left. I certainly know the perfect way to make a first impression. Rocco was the only one who wasn't laughing at me. He simply smiled his gorgeous smile and winked at me over his shoulder as he left.

"Mishap? What kind of mishap?" Matt enquires. I close my eyes tightly. I'm going to have to tell Matt everything, and there is only one thought going through my mind at this particular moment. *Please don't fire me!*

"Well, the thing is … I accidentally set off the fire alarm from the computer and the whole place had to be evacuated. But, I apologised and everyone told me that it was okay and understood that it's my first day." I explain quickly, without having any time to even take a breath. I needed to get my explanation out before he interrupted me.

"The whole place got evacuated? How could you do that Makenzie? Do you understand what would have happened if …?" With that last word, Matt bursts into a fit of laughter. *What the hell?* He must see the look washing over my face change, from panic to confusion because he's trying to control his laughter, but he's failing miserably at it.

"I'm sorry, Makenzie. I'm just pulling your leg. I heard from a few of the guys what had happened and I couldn't resist playing with you," I look at him with complete shock now. He's only having a joke with me?

"You knew? And you still had me explain it? You are such a horrible man, Matt!" I shout at him. I can't believe he just got me like that. I feel a drop of sweat rolling down my spine from the panic he's just made me feel.

"I'm sorry, I'm sorry! Rocco said that it would be funny, and it would make you feel better if I teased you about it. Honestly, the amount of times that I've set that bloody thing off doesn't bear thinking about," Matt explains, though the only words I seem to be able to comprehend are when he mentions that Rocco said he should do it. That sneaky little … I will get him back for this!

"As long as no harm has been done, Matt. I really need this job and don't want to do anything stupid enough to lose it."

"You're doing great. Honestly, Makenzie, you've made my job so much easier, so as long as you don't burn the place down then your job is quite safe."

It's nice to hear Matt say that. It has set me at ease, especially after the morning I've had. Note to self, though. Don't burn the pool down, you know, just if I want to keep my job.

Chapter Three

Thankfully the rest of my day passed by without any more problems, and I was ready to leave on time at 1pm, when the late shift receptionist, Lucy, arrived. She is older than me but not by much and she seems really nice. She has blonde hair and a very infectious laugh, the people that come to the pool must love her.

Once we've completed the hand over and say goodbye, I leave through the main doors, dreaming of the taste of a proper caramel mocha with lots of added whipped cream from the local coffee shop. I think I'm entitled to indulge in a reward for having made it through my entire first day, especially after the way that it started out. I haven't splurged on a proper cup of coffee recently, but today I definitely think I deserve to treat myself.

I'm walking down the next street over, and suddenly I become aware of someone walking very close behind me. Way too close for comfort. This person obviously hasn't ever heard of giving people their personal space. I turn around, ready to tell the person to move back, but pause in my tracks when I come face to face with that gorgeous smile that I'm getting so used to seeing. I'm pretty sure that I could gaze at his smile all day long, though, at the moment, I'm still fuming about the Matt thing, so I turn away from him and continue walking down the street.

"Hey, wait up! Am I not even gonna get a hello?" He asks and breaks into a jog until he catches up to me.

"A hello? You're lucky you're not getting a punch in the nose at this moment in time." I answer him with a deceptively calm voice.

"Wait. Why are you mad at me this time?" Rocco asks in an annoyingly innocent voice. Does he honestly think that I don't know what he did? I stop in the middle of the pavement, which makes him still as well, and I look back at him.

"I had a chat with Matt. A chat where your name just so happened to come up in the conversation."

"Oh." At least he has the decency to look a little bit ashamed. He's looking down at his feet, and I'm trying so hard not to giggle at him. He looks like a kid who just got caught with his hand in the cookie jar.

"Yes, oh! I mean, you didn't think that I'd been through enough today already without you thinking it would be the funniest thing in the world for my boss to pretend to be angry with me?"

"I swear I didn't tell him to do it ... Okay, well, maybe I did in an around about way. But I promise that after I did I told him not to as you'd had a bad enough day." He pleads with me as I begin to walk away from him and towards the coffee shop, but I can hear he's still following behind me. Reaching the entrance door and pulling it open, I look back at him and see that he's throwing me his best puppy dog eyes. I need to stay strong. I'm not letting him get away with it that easily. I step inside and join the queue, pretending to be too engrossed in the menu on the wall to say anything else. He steps closer behind me, so close that I can feel the heat radiating from his body as he whispers in my ear,

"Let me buy your coffee. Let me say I'm sorry." Goosebumps begin to appear all over my body as his breath slides over my ear and neck. I quickly close my eyes in an attempt to hide the effect he's having on me.

How can his closeness make me feel like this? He hasn't even touched me, but I feel as though he's just run his hot hands all over my body. I'm so aware of him presence, though I'm not sure if I want to step closer to him or move further away.

"Are you going to order today, love?" The lady behind the counter bellows down the line at me. Or I should say, where the line *was* before I retreated into my daydream about having Rocco's hands on me.

"Um, yeah. I'll have a large caramel mocha with whipped cream to take away, please." I'm trying to act as though I didn't just make a fool of myself in front of Rocco ... *again*. Standing off to the side a little so that Rocco can give his order to the girl, I desperately try not to look at him.

"I'll have an iced tea with no added sugar to go, please. I'll pay for both." Rocco tells the lady behind the counter. When I look up at him, I see that he's smiling right back at me.

"Please let me pay? I want to say that I'm sorry. Maybe we can take them over to the park and sit and talk. I feel like I know you, but I really don't."

"Ok, I think I can do that. But I'm not forgiving you ... *yet.*" I answer earning another smile from him as he hands the money over, paying for the drinks. He moves to stand beside me as we wait for our drinks to be made. He seems to be happy with himself. He looks devilishly handsome when he smiles. I catch myself before I begin to daydream again and turn away to watch my mocha being made.

"Don't you find that stuff sweet and sickly and gross?" I throw him a questioning look, there is no way he can be talking about my coffee.

"Shhhhh...Don't talk like that in front of the mocha. It'll get all upset and cry. And, no. No I don't find it too sweet, 'Mr no added sugar!'"

"Ha ha! Upset the mocha? Really? I think maybe someone has a slight problem with her love for a certain drink." He's having too much fun teasing me, and I know it's not the most grown up approach to an argument, but I stick my tongue out at him anyway. This just makes him laugh harder, and with a slight blush warming me cheeks I turn towards the serving counter again. Thankfully my mocha is ready, so I grab it from the counter and make my way over to the door. I hear him chuckling behind me as I walk back into the street and head over to the park without waiting for him. Serves him right for making fun of me.

I'm already sitting on the park bench relaxing by the time he catches up with me. I notice that he actually looks surprised to see me here as he takes a seat beside me. We're sitting in the shade of the trees, and it's another hot day. I'll take any relief I can before heading home to the oven that is my apartment. We sit together in silence for a few moments, I'm not sure what to say to him now that we're here.

"I didn't think you'd be here. Do you realise you're always mad at me?"

"You just bought me a coffee, so I'm keeping to my side of the deal. And, I'm not always mad at you. A little miffed maybe, but that's because you're always laughing at me. Well, either that or scaring me." It's only now I realise that, through the limited time that I've known him, he has probably scared me more than anyone else before. Maybe it's because I never seem to be able to relax when I'm around him. I'm being unfair to him though, I know I am. It's not his fault that he brings out all of these feelings in me whenever he gets close. The feelings that seem to make me lose the ability to think and to speak.

"So, 'Mr no added sugar', tell me about yourself. What makes Rocco … Rocco?"

"There really isn't much to tell," he shrugs his shoulders as he begins to answer me. "I'm twenty eight years old and I run a company that supplies and fits custom made parts for motorbikes. We have a garage around here, but I'm the suit of the company. I don't like getting my hands dirty." He winks at me when he says the last few words, so I know he's pulling my leg again, but I realise in the few times I've seen him he has never been in a suit. Like now, for example. He's wearing knee length black cargo pants and a long sleeved white shirt. I'm not saying that he doesn't look good, it's just that he doesn't look like a businessman, that's all.

"So you get to wear a suit all day while the grease monkeys do your bidding?" I tease.

"Ha! Yeah. I suppose you could say that. But someone has to go along to the meetings and make the deals. My business partner, Mason, just doesn't do the whole need to be sensible and act like a grown up thing. So, I deal with that part of it all, and he deals with the actual running of the garages. It seems to work well for us."

"Do you work at the garage much yourself?" He seems to spend a lot of time at the pool training, and now he's sitting here and having a coffee with me in the middle of the afternoon. Not that I am complaining having him sit here and have coffee with me, but I would think that his garages would run normal business hours, so I'm just assuming he doesn't go in very often.

"I go in every now and again, just to see how things are going. I'm just getting back into the swing of things after … um, after a break from the company. So, tell me what brings a lovely girl like you to this neck of the woods."

I immediately notice his not so subtle subject change. Being someone who has mastered the art myself since my split with Carl, I can spot them from a mile away. The amount of times I had to avoid questions from well meaning 'friends', I should now be considered a master subject changer. I let him make the change though, because there's obviously something that he doesn't want to openly talk about with me.

"Oh, you know. Age-old situation. Fell in love with a guy, got engaged to him, and then I found out that he's a complete douchebag. And when I found out, your whole world falls apart." I say it with a smile, trying to look as though it doesn't really bother me. I don't need him to know that it still hurts, that simply talking about it can make my heart feel like its breaking again. I don't need Rocco to feel sorry for me, or worse, thinking I'm still pining over my ex. Because no matter how much it still pains me to think of it, there is no way that I want my ex back.

"Wow. Ok, well compared to yours, my life sounds boring now. Care to explain a little further? Only if you want to, though. I wouldn't want to overstep the mark or anything." I smile back at him. He seems like a really sweet guy. It has been such a long time since I just spoke to someone about all this, especially someone who is willing to listen to it and not judge. All my friends had chosen sides after my split with Carl, and it hadn't worked out in my favour, leaving me with very few people to talk to.

"It's nothing, really. I was engaged to my boss after we'd dated for a few years. Everything was great up until I found out that he was also sleeping with his PA, Rose. I think the only reason I found out about her was because she fell pregnant with his baby. So, he left me for her because he has always wanted kids. I lost my fiancé and had to leave my job, as it got awkward. He got to keep the house we lived in because it was all in his name, even though we bought it together … so, anyway. Here I am. In a city that I know hardly anything about, with no friends and living in an apartment that would have fitted into my last closet." I turn to face him now that I've finished the rant about my life and see that his mouth is hanging open and there's shock filtering into his widened eyes. I find the face he's pulling really funny and even though I try my hardest not to burst into laughter, I fail. Sadly, the sound leaving my lips isn't a little lady like giggle. I have tears running down my cheeks, and I let out what has to be the loudest snort possible. He's looking at me as though I'm from another planet, which only sets me off again. I honestly can't remember the last time I laughed like this, and I have to admit that it feels really good to just let go. I try to stop, but every time I look at him, I begin to laugh some more. I'm beginning to think that I may have just completely lost my mind.

"I know what you need." Rocco says the sound of his voice bringing me out from my hysteria. Trying to control both my breathing, and myself I lift my hand up to wipe the tears away from my cheek, but a strong hand beats me to it. Rocco runs his thumb under my eye, catching the tears that are still lying there. As I look into his eyes, a shiver runs through my entire body. It's as though his skin is connected to an electrical circuit, and as he touches me I can feel a current running through from his body and into mine.

"Oh, and what is it you think I need?" I ask with a breathy voice that I can't manage to control.

"A night out. We'll take you and show you what the nightlife this area has to offer. Maybe make you a few new friends along the way, what do you say?" We? Does that mean he has a girlfriend? This is just so typical. The first guy I happen to like since douchebag, and he's taken. I shouldn't be surprised. Guys who look like him aren't ever going to be single for long. The feeling of disappointment that works its way through me shocks

34

me a little, I obviously was hoping for something a little more with him. He bumps me on the arm with his elbow, bringing me away from my thoughts, and I realise that he has still been talking to me.

"Sorry, I zoned out there for a minute," I turn to face him while giving him an apologetic smile. "What were you saying?"

"I was saying that, if you want to, we could meet up at one of the local bars first and then maybe head onto a club or something. It would give you a chance to meet Mason before it gets too loud. How does that sound?"

"So, it would just be the three of us?" I just can't help myself. I need to know if he's seeing anyone.

"Yeah at the bar it will be, but once we reach the club, I can guarantee to you that Mason will hook up with someone and then it'll just be the two of us. If that's ok with you? I mean, I won't abandon you if that's what you're thinking." He's looking at me eagerly and waiting for me to answer him. It's been such a long time since I went and had some fun dancing. Carl wasn't the type of guy who would go to a nightclub. He was more of a go to a wine bar dressed in a suit and discuss the country's economy type of guy. I think this would be a really good night out, and it would also give me a chance to get to know Rocco a little bit more.

"You know what? That's sounds like a lot of fun. When were you thinking?"

"How about Saturday? It'll give you enough time to recover from your first week at work. We can't have you tired and wanting to go home early." He's wearing a cheeky grin as he answers my question. I can't have him thinking that I'll be a party pooper, can I?

"We can do Friday night if you prefer? I'm sure I'll have the energy to cope with anything you guys can throw at me." I smile

35

sweetly and flutter my eyelashes at him. He laughs at my best attempt of trying to look innocent. I've been told a few times before that it's not very convincing, so I'm not surprised by his reaction in the least.

"No, Saturday night would be better for me. I have a meeting in the morning that I really can't afford to be hung-over for, and Mason always seems to be able to get me even more intoxicated than I ever intend to be."

"So, it's not me that won't be able to handle the pressure? And you tried to blame it all on me. Saturday sounds perfect, and I'm looking forward to meeting Mason and finding out how you both show a lady a good time." It's my turn to wink at him, and I manage it just before I begin to laugh again. We sit and talk in the shade a little longer, neither of us seeming eager to leave. I notice how easy it is to talk to him, and I can feel myself beginning to relax around him.

Chapter Four

The rest of my working week flew by so quickly, that I can't believe it's Saturday already. The week seemed to go really well once I'd finally gotten myself settled in. Luckily, everyone has stopped laughing at me about the alarm incident, and I have even managed not to evacuate the pool since.

All the people who use the pool seem nice enough, and they like to stop by the desk for a while and chat, especially the guys from the swim team which only makes my day better. Matt seems happy with how quickly I've picked up everything, and he has even started to give me other jobs to do, such as the billing and invoicing. I think this helps to take the slack off of him a little and considering once this was my area of expertise, no training has been needed.

Right now I'm standing in front of my closet and trying to decide on what to wear. My main problem is that I have no idea what the girls around here wear to the clubs. Short, long, revealing or casual? Why didn't I think to ask someone? I never even thought to ask Lucy before I left work today, I was just so eager to get home and get ready to go out.

I'd originally started by styling my hair, so it was sitting around my shoulders in soft waves, but then I decided to put it up instead. I hate the feeling of it sticking to my back when I'm dancing and sweating, and I plan on dancing a lot tonight. So after using pins to style it on the top of my head, with a few curls falling around my face, and my fringe swept over to the side, I'm happy with how it looks, and I'm pretty sure it should survive for the night.

I recheck the little makeup that I applied earlier, to make sure that it isn't smudged, and then reapply some nude gloss and a little more eyeliner. I've never been overly keen on wearing much makeup. I prefer to just highlight my eyes and lips. I have always been told they are my two best features, so I want them to look their best tonight. Now all that's left for me to do is decide on which dress I'm going to wear.

Red or black? ... Red or black?

I decide on the black dress. It's a halter style dress with a skirt that flares out around the knees. It looks flirty, without appearing cheap. The main reason I love it is because it shows the tattoo at the top of my back, and I love my tattoo. It is a series of black swirls travelling up over the centre of my spine, and at my shoulders is a set of angel wings. Carl had always hated it, but I didn't care and to be perfectly honest, it doesn't matter to me who does or doesn't. All that matters is I love it. I'd gotten it on the day of my eighteenth birthday, as a memory of my little sister Cassie who'd died in a pool accident when she was seven years old. I was twelve at the time and obviously hadn't handled it very well since I still had a fear of water. She'd been swimming in one of our local public pools, and her hair had gotten caught in one of the drains. The pool had been so busy that no one had noticed her until I'd started shouting out for her. The lifeguard's heard me and cleared the entire pool to do a head count, but it had been too late. They found her at the bottom and weren't able to resuscitate her in time. I haven't been able to go near a pool since that day because the memories just won't allow me to. The guilt of her dying when I was supposed to be watching her will haunt me for the rest of my life. This is why I'm not so keen to get any closer to the pool at work, though the job itself has been okay so far. My area is the reception and that where I plan on staying.

I do my final checks in the mirror and realise that if I don't leave soon, I'll be late to meet with the guys. If they move on from the bar, we've arranged to meet in before I arrive then, I'll be completely lost. I spray a final spritz of perfume, grab my denim jacket and purse, and then leave my apartment.

It doesn't take me long to arrive at the bar after following the directions that Rocco had given me when we last spoke to one another. I'm a little bit early and undecided on whether I should go inside or wait by the entrance doors for them. I'd feel really uncomfortable if I had to sit in there on my own for too long. I've never been the type of person who can comfortably walk into a busy bar unless I know there's already someone inside waiting for me. I feel that everyone watches me, watching and waiting to see if anyone else turns up. Paranoid? Yes, but I just can't help it. This is why I always went to a friend's house to get ready, safety in numbers.

After a couple of minutes pass by, I decide to brave it. This is the new me from now on, and I've promised myself that I'll grab life by both hands and hold on for the ride. Taking a deep breath I take the first few steps towards what I hope will be a new start.

I make my way through the small group of people who are crowding the area just inside the doorway, keeping a lookout for Rocco, just in case he's here already. I don't see him, though I do notice a table that's free. I head over, deciding to grab a seat. It's one thing walking into a bar on your own, but it's another thing completely to stand all by yourself by the bar. I remove my jacket, placing it over the back of the chair before sitting down. I choose the seat that's facing the doors so I can watch as people arrive, and always looking out for Rocco.

"Hi there. What's a beautiful girl like yourself doing sitting here all alone?" I turn and see a guy standing right beside me. He's placed one of his arms around the back of my chair, while resting the other on the table in front of me. He's smiling at me, and though I'm sure he's trying to make himself look irresistible, to me he just both looks and sounds like a bit of a creep.

I really hate being hit on by random guys, especially in bars. His face is so close to me now that I can feel his warm breaths sweeping over my face. He's obviously had a fair bit to drink already. His breath smells strongly of beer, though this wouldn't usually bother me, having that accompanied with everything else that this guy is bringing to the table is making me want to heave. I'm really not interested.

"Just waiting on some friends. They should be here any minute now." I answer him as politely as I can before turning away from him. I'm hoping that he'll take my not so subtle hint and leave.

"Well, why don't I just sit right here and keep you company until they arrive?" I'm just about to answer him when I feel a warm hand lightly touching my shoulder. My skin prickles from the touch and I feel a warmth spreading throughout my entire body. I instantly know who it is. Rocco.

"The lady already has company, so why don't you just go and sit somewhere else?" He's practically growling at the guy. I can feel a pull in my stomach as he says the words and my breath begins to hitch. I lift my head to face him and see that he's staring the guy down. His gorgeous eyes are almost glowing with, well I'm not sure, but I'm glad I'm not the guy on the receiving end of his almost deathly glare. The guy mutters an apology under his breath and Rocco removes his hand before sitting beside me. I only just manage to control a moan of complaint that has already made its way halfway up my throat as he removes his hand.

"Now, I will give the guy some credit for noticing how beautiful you look tonight, but I think we'll keep you company instead of him. Sorry, we're late." I smile from his comment, feeling happy at the words he's just spoken. I allow my gaze to drift over Rocco now that he's right in front of me.

He's wearing a pair of dark blue jeans with a black casual shirt, the sleeves rolled up to his forearms. I can see the ends of what looks to be a black tribal tattoo showing from under one sleeve and making its way to his wrist. This is the first time I've noticed that he has a tattoo. How is this something I have missed? He was practically naked the day the alarm went off at the pool. Ok, I admit, I'd been paying more attention to his abs than his arms that day. I love men with tattoos. I had always been hinting to Carl about getting one, but he always said 'people of importance didn't lower themselves by having tattoos', I should have known right then that he wasn't the right guy for me.

I make a mental note to make sure to check out the rest of his tattoo when he's swimming next. I really want to see ... *no*. I'm already having a very overwhelming need to see his tattoo, and adding these thoughts to the already present chemistry between us won't help me control myself. The more I'm finding out about Rocco, the more attracted to him I'm becoming. I manage to tear my eyes away from him when I notice a guy sitting next to him. He must be Mason. He's wearing a huge grin over his face, and I can tell that he's just caught me checking Rocco out. I feel the heat flush up over my neck as it rises into my cheeks, settling there.

"You gonna introduce me to your fine lady, Rocco? Or are you just gonna sit there all night with your tongue hanging out?" His grin dramatically widens as he speaks and is obviously feeling good about making us both feel awkward.

When I had finally brought my eyes over to look at Mason, and I was shocked by what I saw. If two guys could look any more like brothers, without being related, then it would be them. Actually, maybe they are related. Rocco only mentioned that they're best friends, but perhaps they share the same DNA as well. Both have dark, messy hair, the messy style that probably costs a fortune to obtain in some trendy salon. He has the same lean build as Rocco, though he appears to be less muscly in the arms. It's easy to compare them while they're sitting together. Mason is wearing a tight white muscle top with sleeves that end half way down his biceps, also showing a tattoo over his forearm. I'm under no illusion that Mason must have women falling over themselves to gain his attention, and I'm pretty sure he uses it to his full advantage. Rocco's eyes are dark. They look almost black, though they still seem to sparkle brightly when he smiles, while Mason's are a brilliant bright blue. So blue, in fact, they look almost unreal.

"Mason, this is Makenzie. Makenzie, this idiot over here is Mason." I stretch my hand over the table, and I'm surprised when Mason stands up before kissing my hand. I glance over to Rocco and notice that he's beginning to roll his eyes. I have a funny feeling that tonight, with these two guys, is going to be ...shall we say interesting?

"It's completely my pleasure, pretty thing. I see that our guy Rocco over here had been completely underselling you when he said you were gorgeous." I sneak a peek over at Rocco and find him glaring at Mason with a pinkish tinge appearing over his cheeks. I'm feeling rather delighted to find out that he thinks I'm gorgeous, but I'm not so sure he wanted me to know if the look he's throwing Mason is anything to go by.

"So, what can I get you to drink, sexy?" Mason asks me as he stands from his seat.

"I'll have a midori and lemonade, please. With lots of ice." He's looking at me rather strangely, as though I've just spoken in a foreign language or something.

"A what? Just a midori and lemonade? So, not some girlie cocktail that'll make me grow boobs as soon as I go to order it?" he jokes. I know it isn't exactly the strongest of drinks, but I don't really like the taste of alcohol, so this is a good drink for me. It's sweet and doesn't taste as though it has any alcohol in it.

"No girly cocktail. Just midori and lemonade. Do I need to go and get it for myself?" I make it look as though I'm about to stand, but Mason catches me by the elbow and pushes me back into my seat.

"No, no. I'm going. You wanting the usual, mate?" Rocco nods a yes, and I watch as Mason begins to walk away. My eyes stay on him as he approaches the bar and as he starts talking to the girl standing on the other side. She certainly appears happy to have his full attention.

"He's not exactly the best guy if you hope to have something more than just a casual fling."

"What?" I ask turning my attention back over to Rocco. What he's just said has me feeling slightly confused. I mustn't have heard him right.

"Mason. He's a great guy and a great friend, but he isn't serious boyfriend material." Okay, and now I'm even more confused. Mason and a relationship? Is he suggesting Mason and me?

"I saw the way you looked at him when he walked over to the bar just now." I feel as though I've just slipped into an alternative universe. A place where I don't understand anything that's going on. Or, maybe it's Rocco who has taken something.

"I honestly have no idea what you're talking about, Rocco. Why would I have any interest in Mason? I've only just met him."

"I'm just guessing. I'm used to women following him around. They're always interested in him. I mean, I can understand, he's a good-looking guy and knows exactly the right things to say to them. I suppose that he's hard to resist that's all." I almost laugh at him, but I know he's only trying to be truthful about his thoughts. He honestly thinks that it's Mason who's irresistible? I see the woman around him all the time, checking him out. The girls behind the counter in the coffee shop that I go to after work fight with each other over who gets to serve him. He must know he's gorgeous. Does he not own a mirror?

"Well, I can tell you right now that I honestly have no interest in Mason. He's not the reason I'm here tonight." I suddenly realise what I've just said to him, and now I'm beginning to feel a little awkward. The way that we're looking at each other in this moment and from the way his face seems to be holding some kind of hope, it's as though he wants to believe what I'm saying but can't. I try to recover quickly from the awkwardness.

"Besides, you'll find out for yourself pretty soon, that I'm not like most of the other girls. A pretty face isn't everything. I'm a woman of substance." I can't resist throwing a small wink at him. At least this action seems to be making him lose the look that's just taken over his features. He was looking as though someone had just stolen his new teddy bear, though now replacing it is a smile that's tugging at the side of his lips.

"Here we go people. Let's make a toast to the night ahead." Mason says as he places our drinks down on the table in front of us. I take my drink in my hand, feeling happy to have a distraction from the strange conversation that was just going on between Rocco and me. Raising his drink up and looking at the both of us expectantly, Mason waits until we've raised our glasses up to meet his.

"To new friends." I move to clink my glass to his, but he pulls it back away before I have the chance. He gives me a look that I imagine is meant to be a glare, but it's not very convincing.

"I'm not finished!" He laughs and so I move my glass back close to me and smile at him apologetically, humouring him.

"To new friends. May they be everything we hope they are, and perhaps even a little more. And, here's to Mason getting a little action tonight." He clinks glasses with us as I let a very audible groan out. Yeah, this night is definitely going to be an interesting one.

I don't think I'm going to be able to keep up with the guys because they're drinking so much. We're just leaving through the exit of the third bar as we make our way to the nightclub, and I'm already feeling as though I've passed my alcohol limit. In fact, I think I passed that limit about five drinks ago, and if I drink any more tonight, I might not be able to last much longer. My head is spinning, I feel like the world is spinning faster than normal, and I can't keep up.

I keep telling myself that dancing will help me to sober me up a bit. No more alcohol, just dancing. Seeing as though the club isn't very far away from the bar we were just in, we've decided to walk there, and I've come to the conclusion that my choice of footwear for this evening isn't exactly the best for walking any sort of distance. Add into that equation that I've consumed way too much alcohol, and it's a recipe for disaster. While the world continues to spin, I become aware of how unsteady on my feet I am. I'm needing to concentrate so hard on making sure that my feet go forward, one in front of the other, that I don't even notice the group of guys that are heading our way. That's until one bumps my shoulder with his, knocking my balance way off course. I'm suddenly all too aware of what's about to happen.

The bump spins my body around, though my upper body manages to move quicker than my feet can manage. I'm now just praying that the alcohol in my system will stop the pain that I'm inevitably going to feel when I hit the pavement. I close my eyes and wait for the impact, but it never comes.

A strong pair of arms wraps themselves around my waist and grab me up before I can land in a very unladylike heap on the ground. I can hear someone shouting somewhere, but all I can focus on is the hard chest that I've just been pulled tightly up against. From the reaction my body is having to the connection with this body, I know who has a hold of me. Even in my intoxicated state, my body is alight with awareness of his body and touch. He's like a hard wall. A wall of pure male. His arms are so strong that I can feel his muscles ripple as he holds my body to his. I close my eyes, it's the only way I'm going to survive being so close to him.

"Makenzie? Are you ok? Why isn't she answering, Rocco? Did she hit something?" Masons voice filters through my ears and my brain finally begins to function properly again.

I open my eyes, and I'm now gazing into the worried eyes of Mason. I wonder how long I've been standing here in Rocco's arms, acting as though I have no brain.

"I'm fine … Don't worry about me … It just took me by surprise, that's all. I was pretty sure that I was gonna end up on my arse." Once I'm sure that I've fully regained my balance, I pull myself away, out of Rocco's arms. I turn slowly to face him, hoping that he can't see the look of attraction that's bound to be showing in my eyes.

"Thank you. That could have hurt … *a lot!*" His eyes appear very dark as I speak, not just because we're under some streetlights and that they're creating shadows, but I'm sure that I can see a look of longing and lust within his. I hope it's not the alcohol that's making me see things. I would hate to think that I was the only one affected by our encounter just now. I can still feel the warmth of his arms around me. I shake my head and try not to think about it anymore.

"You're welcome. Can't have you breaking your butt on our first night out, can we?" He answers, as though he's trying to make light of the situation in hand.

"Well, let's get moving shall we? The drunk girl nearly ended up on her ass, so it's definitely time to dance!" I would say just about anything at this time to try and get us all moving again. I need something to distract me from the feelings in my body that I can't seem to control.

"Yes! The drunk girl has spoken so let's go and get another drink!" Mason says with a wink. Oh God, not more alcohol …

Chapter Five

The club's a lot smaller than I'd expected it to be, though it's really crowded in here. I'm only barely able to squeeze past the party revellers so I can follow Mason to wherever it is that he's leading us.

I know that Rocco's right behind me, so at least I know that I'm not going to get lost in here, no matter how much I'm knocked around. The crowd begins to thin as we make our way into a seating area. It's surprising how quiet it is in this section, and as I look around, I notice that most of the tables are empty.

"Why is it so quiet here?" I lean over and almost shout into Mason's ear. He's stopped ahead of me and is talking to what looks to be a waitress. If I'm to be completely truthful here, it's hard to tell by what little clothing she's actually wearing, but the white apron around her waist kind of gives her away.

"That's because this is the VIP area. You know only the best for your first night out." I turn quickly to look at Rocco, so I can try and figure out whether Mason is telling the truth or not. I haven't known him for long, but I've already worked out that he likes to be a bit of a joker. He has this cheeky bad boy charm about him.

"Yes it is. But, what he's not telling you is that he has a pass to get us in here because he 'knows' the owners daughter." When he says the word 'knows', he uses his fingers and makes air quotes, making it very clear that we're now standing in this area only because of some sexual favour Mason has done, or is planning to do. I'm now beginning to feel a little bit grossed out about being in here.

I stay standing where I am and look around the club. I need a distraction, any distraction to stop me thinking about Mason's loose morals. I hear 'Dirty Dancer by Enrique' beginning to play. I love this song. Watching the people on the dance floor, I feel my body automatically beginning to sway along with the beat. All I've thought about all might is dancing, but now the option is here, I'm starting to feel very self-conscious. When I used to go out, I was usually surrounded by a group of friends, and right now dancing on my own isn't something that I want to do. I need to stop before I embarrass myself. Just as I still my movements, I feel a hard body move up behind me.

With lips brushing my ear he asks, "Do you like to dance?" I momentarily lose the ability to think about anything that he's just said. I hear him chuckle deeply in my ear and know that he's fully aware of what he causes me to feel when he's this close to me. Is he doing this on purpose?

"I love to dance. Though dancing alone is something that I don't do. There will never be enough alcohol in the world for that to happen."

"Who said you would be dancing alone?" I feel his hand moving over to my hips, and he begins to squeeze me gently as he pulls me back against his body. I can feel the warmth spreading out from his hand and feel tingles spreading to my core.

I close my eyes as I try to fight against all of the sensations that are invading my body. All I can concentrate on is him. The heat of his body against my back. The warmth of his hand on my hip. His breath against the side of my neck, which is now causing goose bumps to appear all over my body.

I love his smell. It's fresh and clean, almost like the ocean, but underlying there's still a faint smell of the chlorine from the pool. It's so uniquely *him*. I take another deep breath and let his scent invade my senses. It's so unique that I feel as though I'm drowning in it. I crave to run my nose up his neck to feast on him some more.

My eyes flash open when the reality sets in. I'm actually becoming turned on by the smell of chlorine. Since when did I stop associating chlorine with negative thoughts? I've spent most of my life fearing the smell, and now I desire it? I need to move away from him. I need to get some space so I can clear my mind.

I try to move away from his chest, but his hand moves from my hip and across my stomach, pulling me back some more and even closer to him. His hips begin to move in time with the music, and I feel myself automatically melting into his arms. I can't seem to be able to pull myself away. I start to sway with him, letting him guide my movements, while resting my head back on his shoulder. He moves his nose down, nuzzling into the crook of my neck.

My breathing becomes laboured, and I can feel a drop of sweat running between my breasts as we continue to move. I begin to feel light headed and as much as I would like to blame the alcohol, I know that this time it isn't. It's him. It's all him. Being close to him like this is making my body react in a way that I never thought possible. I've never experienced feelings like this before, and I didn't know that it would ever be possible to feel this alive.

His lips brush tenderly against my neck, causing a moan to leave involuntarily from my lips. I can't help it. All I can feel are warm tingles all over my body from the way his body is moulding with mine. I feel the muscles deep within my core beginning to tighten, and I know that it shouldn't be possible just from this very simple contact between us.

I'm hoping the loud music is covering the uncontrollable noises that are now escaping from deep within me. I grind back into his body, getting carried away from the feel of his hard chest against me. He's like steel though he's warm and comfortable. I can't seem to get close enough to him.

I lean my head over to the side a little when I feel him brushing his nose over my skin. Doing this has given him access to my full throat, and that's when I feel his tongue beginning to lick the bottom edge of my ear. He pulls my lobe into his mouth and nibbles down gently before soothing it with his tongue. My body feels as though it's about to spontaneously combust at any given moment. The need that's raging through me right now is making me feel as though his actions are more than I can possibly handle. I reach my hand behind me and stroke my fingers leisurely through Rocco's hair, but our connection is broken when he's pushed from behind. I feel flustered, almost as though what just happened didn't really happen and that I'm beginning to wake up from a dream. *A very welcome dream.*

"You guys are looking very cosy over here." Mason says while raising his eyebrows at the two of us. This earns him a punch to the arm from Rocco. I'm debating whether I should give him one as well for interrupting the moment.

"I'm just going to use the gents. I won't be long." I watch Rocco as he walks away and notice that he's shaking his head. I know that I haven't been on the dating scene for a very long time, but I can't imagine that his reaction is a good sign.

I go back over and sit at our table. There's a jug of iced water in the middle, and I pour myself a glass. Mason has just tried to encourage me to have something stronger, but I know that I really need to stop drinking for the rest of the night. It's messing with my self-control. The cold water is helping to cool my inner temperature, which is great considering that it needs to be drastically cooled.

Rocco still hasn't come back out from the gents, and I'm starting to feel a bit weird about sitting here on my own. It's not as though I know anyone so I can go and strike up a conversation while I wait for him to return. I sit and watch Mason as he talks with yet another woman. I think this one is number three of the night. I have a little giggle to myself when I think back to our earlier conversation, when Rocco honestly thought that it was Mason I was interested in.

As I continue to watch, I see that they're looking very cosy over there together. But then, he has looked that way with all of them so far. Yes. He is most definitely a player. I continue to watch Mason and see him reaching for his phone. He stares at the screen for a minute or so before looking over in my directions, and then proceeds to tap away at a few keys. After replacing his mobile phone back into his pocket, he walks over to me and leans close enough so I can hear him over the loud music that's playing out.

"Rocco's gone home."

"What?" I'm pretty sure I must have heard him wrong. Rocco went to the toilet.

"I just got a text from him. He said that something came up, and he needed to leave. He asked me to get you home safe."

I can't believe that he left! I only came out tonight because of him. He's the one who'd invited me to come out and have some fun, not the other way around.

"Are you being serious? He just left without even saying goodbye?" Mason nods once at me. I stand abruptly and gather my purse and jacket, suddenly I don't feel so drunk anymore.

I brush past Mason and begin to make my way across the dance floor. How could a great night go downhill so fast? I thought that we were all having fun, I know that I was.

I exit the nightclub without noticing, and I'm so mad at Rocco. I feel stupid and let down. Why invite me out, dance with me like he did and then leave without even so much as a goodbye? He said he wouldn't leave me alone. He knew that Mason would leave us for someone. He promised that he'd stay with me!

"God damn it, Makenzie! Would you slow down?" I turn to see Mason running down the street as he tries to catch up with me. It's only at this point that I notice in my anger that I've walked past all the taxi cabs outside the club, and I'm getting further away from any other signs of life.

"Where the hell do you think you're going?"

"I'm going home. I just need to go home and sleep." I struggle to keep the sob that I feel at the back of my throat at bay. I don't want to look like an even bigger loser right now. Mason had seen us dancing together and saw what was happening between us. Then Rocco left. Mason must think that I'm the biggest loser ever, managing to chase him away like that.

"Come back this way. I'll get you a taxi and make sure you get home okay." He gently places his hand on my arm and pulls me back towards the club. I'm thankful that he'd caught up with me before I ended up somewhere I didn't recognise. Mason opens the door to the first taxi in the line, just outside of the club and talks with the driver. He then removes his wallet from his back pocket and hands some money over.

"Mason, I can pay my own way home." I begin to protest.

"Listen, Mackenzie. Rocco invited you out with us tonight, and he would be upset to know that I hadn't seen that you got home safely. Just tell the driver where you need to go and then get yourself to bed." He opens the door fully and steps back to allow me inside. I step towards the door of the taxi, and just before I bend to get into the seat, Mason touches me gently on the arm again. I turn to look at him and see the serious look washing over his face.

"Don't judge him too hard, Makenzie." I see the look of remorse crossing over his face. I feel bad for him, especially since Rocco has left him to deal with this situation. A situation that isn't his to deal with. I can feel tears beginning to burn in the back of my eyes. I can't let them fall, not in front of Mason. I think he's dealt with me enough tonight already.

"He's been through a lot in the last few years and he's only now becoming the Rocco he used to be. Give him time. He really is an amazing guy once you get to know him properly. It's just ..." He sighs as he seems to be struggling to find the right words to say to me. "As I say, he's been through a lot. I can't say anymore because it's not my story to tell. Just, just please give him the time he needs. I know he likes you and maybe that's the problem. Ever since ... shit! Look have a safe journey home, and I really hope that we'll see each other again." He runs his hands through his hair while appearing increasingly agitated.

I have no idea why, and I don't know what story there is to tell, but I'm feeling more tired and the alcohol I drank earlier on in the evening is beginning to make things feel a little fuzzy again. I lean over and place a kiss on his cheek.

"Thanks Mason. Go and enjoy the rest of your night, and don't do anything I wouldn't do." That earns me a smile that lights up his eyes.

"Oh, I plan on doing a lot more than that." He raises his eyebrows suggestively a couple of times at me. With that thought now in my head, I lower myself onto the seat as he closes the door for me.

I can't even begin to process everything that's happened tonight, and I'm not even going to try to just now. I lean my head against the back of the seat and close my eyes, finally allowing the alcohol to take its full hold on me.

Chapter Six

Reaching my hand out from underneath my duvet, I desperately try to quiet the incessant ringing that's sounding out from my alarm clock. It can't possibly be time to get up already?

I grab the alarm and bring it closer to me, hoping that I maybe set it for the wrong time or something. Nope. No such luck. It's telling me that it's 4 o'clock, which means that it really is time to get myself out of bed.

It has been over twenty-four hours since I last had a drink, so why is it that I'm still suffering from the after effects? I spent the entire day yesterday laying on the couch and trying not to move too much.

Every time that I even tried to move, I honestly felt as though I was either going to bring up everything I hadn't eaten all day, or felt like my head was going to actually explode. I tried so hard not to think about a certain good-looking guy who had asked me out for the night. The same one who had then left me in the club, feeling like an idiot, because thoughts of him consuming my mind weren't helping to soothe my headache.

I have absolutely no idea what happened. I mean, one minute we were dancing and getting along, let's just say very well, but then in the next I was left standing on my own, with only his best friend there to make sure that I got home safely.

Mason had been great after I left the nightclub and he also text me when I left in the taxi to make sure that I got home okay. Then he messaged me again yesterday, so he could check on me and to make sure that I wasn't suffering too much. He told me that he hadn't managed to get a hold of Rocco because he wasn't answering his phone. So, I'm still none the wiser as to why he just vanished at the end of the night or why it had ended the way it did. Though, I'm pretty sure that Mason knows the reason, he's his best friend after all, but he doesn't tell me or give me any clues as to why.

I throw the duvet cover away from my body and let out a groan. Maybe taking this job wasn't such a great idea. No. No, it was the drinking and going out with him at all that was the bad idea,

Such a bad, bad idea!

I climb in the shower and turn the water temperature up as high as it will possibly go. The muscles down through my neck and in my back begin to relax as the water splashes over me, and I lean both of hands onto the wall, hanging my head down low.

My thoughts soon start to drift, and before I know it, images of dark eyes flashing into my mind begin to make my body spark to life. I groan out loud and shake my head. It would be nice if I could at least stop myself from thinking about Rocco for at least an hour out of my day. He doesn't want me. He's made that perfectly clear both to me, and to almost everyone else who was in the club. It really must take a special skill to be able to scare a guy off just by dancing up close with him. Maybe I should teach classes on it, make a little extra money.

I start washing my hair, determined not to spend any more of my time dwelling on him and how much I must have repulsed him. It was only one night, and nothing really happened between us anyway. There's lots of guys out there, and I'm sure that I'll find another guy that makes my body feel the way Rocco does eventually.

Once I'm done in the shower, I dress in my uniform, tie my hair back, grab my trusty travel mug and make my way to work.

****

I arrive in the building just a couple of minutes before my shift starts, so I don't really have the time to check on the swimmers like I usually do in the morning. I head straight behind my desk and prepare myself, getting ready to start my shift for the day.

I get caught up on the paperwork that Matt left for me on my desk. Apparently the weekend staff don't do paperwork, and before I know it, I hear the door to the opening up and watch as the swimming team begin to leave.

"Good morning, Makenzie." Josh, a member of the swim team says cheerily. Josh seems like a nice guy. He has sandy blonde hair and an easy smile.

"Hey, Josh. How are things?" I glance up at the clock, not believing that it's time for them to leave already. I realise that I'm right. They're finishing up fifteen minutes earlier than normally do. I know it doesn't seem a lot of time, but I judge my shift duties on the time they finish up their training and leave the building.

"They're good. Did you have a good weekend?" He stops just in front of the desk, resting his elbows on the top as he asks, while throwing me a smile.

"Yeah, I did. I went out for the night on Saturday, so that was pretty great, and then on Sunday, well, Sunday wasn't as much fun!" I say while screwing up my nose, which shows him that that day sucked for me. This causes him to laugh lightly.

"Aren't you guys finished up earlier than normal today? Is everything ok in the pool?" I begin to worry that maybe the pool was too cold or something. I lean over the computer to check the readings while I wait for him to answer me.

"Yeah, everything's fine. We finished up with the lanes a bit earlier because Rocco isn't here, that's all. We all managed to get our own lane for a change."

Josh is oblivious to the fact that what he just told me, has my stomach churning and that he may have just broken my heart a little bit. I try really hard to hide the disappointment I'm feeling from knowing Rocco isn't in the building. It's one thing to leave the nightclub because of me, but to miss his practice is a huge crush to the ego. Does he honestly want to avoid me this much that he'd miss training with the team?

I need to stop this. It is time for me to stop wasting my time and energy thinking about Rocco. If he hadn't made it clear enough before, well then he certainly has now. I get it. He doesn't like me. At least, not in the way I'd hoped.

"Hey Makenzie, I've been meaning to ask you something ... I was wondering if you'd maybe like to get dinner one night, you know, just the two of us?" Josh is starting to appear slightly embarrassed as he asks me, though I'm actually finding it quite sweet. My first thought is to thank him but decline, but for some reason I stop myself before the words leave my mouth. Why would I say no? I'm single and new to the area, so why not go out with him and have a little fun in the process? He seems like a nice enough guy, and it's not as though anyone else has asked me to go out on a date with them. Okay, so maybe they have, but I sent him running to the hills, didn't I? Maybe this is just the boost of confidence my ego needs.

"Sure, I'd like that. Thanks ... So, when would you like to go?"

"How about this coming Friday? If you give me your number then I can message you the details once I get a table booked" I smile and reel of my mobile number and watch him as he puts it into his phone. He looks really excited. Less than a minute passes by and a new message comes through. It's a text from him with a smiley face.

"And, now you have mine." He says with a smile as he walks backwards and out through the doors, waving before turning and going completely out from my view.

I sit back in my seat with a smile beginning to cross over my lips. I'm actually quite looking forward to going out and having dinner with him. Okay, I'll admit that my body doesn't react in quite the same to him as it does when I'm near or around Rocco, but that doesn't mean to say that this is a bad thing.

Damn. I was so close to going a whole hour without thinking about him.

****

Finishing up my shift, I leave the pool and make my way slowly towards the coffee shop. Grabbing a coffee from there has become a part of my daily routine. I just can't resist their caramel mochas, though I've stopped getting the whipped cream added on it every time I order. I don't want to end up the size of a house. Today, though, definitely feels like a whipped cream kind of day. I smile inwardly to myself when I realise that I'll use any excuse to add whipped cream on the top.

Making my way inside the cafe, I look over the menu on the wall, just like I do every day, even though I know exactly what I'm going to order. I then approach the girl behind the counter and place my drink order. Is it just me or is she looking at me rather strangely?

"Sorry, is your name Makenzie?" She asks. Her question has me feeling uncomfortable, and I just stand and look at her questioningly. How on earth does she know my name?

"I'm sorry, but do I know you?" She smiles at me as she begins to prepare my coffee. Putting a lid on the top, she pushes it over the counter towards me and smiles again.

"No, you don't. But, he told me that you'd come in at around this time and order a caramel mocha." What? Who told her this? I'm so confused right now.

"I'm sorry. I don't understand. Who told you this? And, *why* did he tell you this?" I feel my eyebrow's furrowing and a frown forming over my mouth.

"I don't know who he is. All he said was that you would come in to get a coffee at around this time. He's already paid for it and told me to make sure you got it." She pushes my coffee even closer to me. I'm pretty sure she just wants me to grab the cup, stop asking her questions and leave.

"Ok, so let me get this straight. A guy came in and bought me a coffee when I wasn't even here? Well, what did he look like? Did he give you a name?" I'm sure that I'm going to get a headache from trying to understand all of this. Why would someone come in and buy me a coffee? And, why not be here to buy me it for himself? Also, how did they even know that I would be here? I know I come here every day, but knowing that someone knows my daily routine is starting to freak me out. There are so many question's that I need answers for.

"I don't know what he looked like. It was Sarah on the other shift that took the message. *See.*" She picks up a piece of paper from behind the counter and holds it up to me. There it is in black and white. A note telling her that, at 1.15pm, a brunette would come in to order a caramel mocha, her name is Makenzie, and the drink has already been paid for.

61

"Oh, okay. Well, em … thanks … *I think.*" I would usually be more worried about accepting the coffee, but I watched her make it myself. I take it from the counter top and then leave.

I make my way over to the park, deciding to sit down for a little while and watch the world pass by. This part of the day has also become a part of my daily routine. I love to just sit and think, or rather, *not think*.

The weather has cooled slightly over the past week, so it feels much more comfortable to be outside. Last week I wasn't able to sit out much longer than thirty minutes before the heat became far too much for me to bear. I stay here for well over an hour, thinking about everything and trying to gather my thoughts. Who on earth went out of their way to buy me a coffee? I think about my date with Josh, and of course, Rocco. I always think about Rocco. *Damn the man.*

The rest of the week passed by, and I followed my usual routine. Rocco hadn't shown up for practice for the entire week, and every time I went to grab a coffee from the coffee shop, there was a caramel mocha with whipped cream waiting for me, at the same time every day. I'd spent so much time wondering about who was buying them for me that I even asked Josh, even though I knew it wasn't him. Then I think, maybe its Rocco. But I think that's more wishful thinking than anything. I begin to wonder when I'll find out who has been buying them for me. It must be someone who knows me and it shouldn't be too hard to figure out, I have a very limited list of friends around here, after all. I feel confident that I'll find out who it is eventually. I mean, is there really any point in buying them for me if they have no intention on me finding out who they are? The other thing that stayed constant the entire week was that but trying not to think about Rocco automatically made me think of him. Between the coffee thing and him not turning up to his swimming, he has been on my mind the entire week.

Tonight is my date with Josh. He messaged me earlier and told me that we're going to be dining in a local Chinese restaurant, which he swears serves the best food that I will ever try in my life. Considering I'm such a huge fan of Chinese food, I'm feeling even more excited about my date with him.

I decided to wear my favourite maxi dress with some flat sandals. I want to feel comfortable, and since Josh isn't overly tall, I don't need to wear heels and make myself even taller. I've kept my makeup to a minimum again, opting for my usual mascara and lip gloss and chose to leave my hair down, only pinning it up on one side with a flower clip which perfectly matches the flowers on my dress.

I hear a knock on the front door. That must be him now. I take one last glance at myself in the mirror, spray some perfume quickly, grab my shawl and then make my way over to greet him. When I open up the door, I see Josh standing on the other side and holding a rather large bouquet of flowers in his hands as he flashes me a smile.

"Wow, Makenzie! You look … just … wow!" he says, which makes me blush a little from the compliment.

"Thanks, and so do you. You look very handsome tonight, Josh." And he really does. His blonde hair is brushed back and away from his face, showing the definition of his cheekbones more than usual. I'm used to seeing him after his swimming training, and it's usually falling down over his eyes.

He's wearing black trousers, accompanied with a white short sleeved buttoned up shirt. I keep waiting for the butterflies to start flying around my stomach, but they never arrive. I'm sure that once we're out I'll start to feel at least *something*. Yes. Once we talk some more, and I'm more relaxed I'm sure I'll feel it then. I accept the flowers from him and place them on the table that's just on the inside of the door, making a mental note to put them in some water when I arrive home later.

"They're beautiful, Josh. Thank you so much, but you really didn't need to bring me anything."

"Oh, shush. I wanted to at least get my beautiful date some flowers." He flashes me the most amazing smile and offers his elbow over in my direction, allowing me to take it.

Still no butterflies.

Chapter Seven

When we arrive at the restaurant, we're seated at a table that's in one of the corners where it's quieter. It's a beautiful place and not what I'd been expecting at all. They have stunning Chinese lanterns hanging from the ceiling, and there's Chinese symbols printed all over the walls. It isn't quite the romantic place that I thought Josh might have taken me to for our first date together. At least I'm thinking of this as our first date, that has to be a good sign? I must like him more than I'd originally thought. We're handed our menus when the waitress comes over to take our drinks order. I decide to order myself an iced tea, and since we'd walked here, Josh orders himself a beer.

"So, tell me, what dish would you recommend?" I ask Josh as I browse over the menu while trying to decide on what to have to eat. I think it may have the most choices I have ever seen on one menu before.

"It's all great. How about we get a banquet menu to share? That way we know there'll be something that we both like and you can try a few different things at the same time?"

"That sounds like a great idea. I'll warn you now, though, when it comes to Chinese food, I can eat my entire body weights worth." I laugh lightly with a smile, feeling very comfortable in his company.

"I highly doubt that with your figure! Though, I guess I'll take my chances." He throws me a wink, along with a huge smile, one that makes the dimples in his cheeks stand out a lot more. The look he's giving me makes him look even more attractive, but I still can't help but notice the fact that he isn't making my body light up in the same way that …no. No. I refuse to allow my mind to wander there right now, especially while I'm on a date. It's not only unfair on me, it's also not fair on Josh. The waitress comes back over to take our food order, and then she leaves us to chat while we wait for our food to arrive.

"So, what brings you to this town of all places, Makenzie? Most people I know can't wait to leave."

"I just needed a change of scenery, that's all. You know what they say, a change is as good as a holiday." It doesn't escape my notice that I'm not entirely forthcoming with the real reason I moved here. I've nothing to hide, but I feel the excuse I just used flowed from my mouth with such a great ease. It's strange because I had no problem sharing my crappy past with Rocco the other day.

"And your change led you here? I mean, don't get me wrong, I'm not complaining that you moved here, it just seems a bit strange that you'd move somewhere where you don't know anyone." He shrugs his shoulders once and gives me another smile. I do think that I can trust him enough to be able to share my life stories with him, just not this one. I'm about to answer his question with another vague answer, but I'm interrupted when the waitress brings our food over to the table. There's a huge variety of food and the serving dishes just keep coming and coming. I begin to laugh, and my laughter only becomes louder as more dishes are set out in front of us.

"Well, you did say you could eat a lot, didn't you?" Josh is trying to keep a straight face while the food just keeps piling up, taking up every available inch on the table.

"Yes … *thankfully.*" I giggle back at him.

Josh was absolutely right; the food here is amazing. I've tried so many new things, and I now feel as though I'm ready to explode. I had a great time trying a little bit of everything. I fed

Josh some of the food from the dishes on my side of the table, and he fed me some from over on his. It should have felt quite intimate, feeding each other, but there just didn't seem to be anything there.

He feels like a friend to me. Nothing more. Maybe I'm being unfair towards Josh, but I'm honestly trying to relax and just go along with the date. I still think that maybe this could possibly go somewhere, but only if I can erase the attraction I feel towards Rocco from my mind. Butterflies whizzing around your stomach from the sight or touch of someone you find attractive aren't always needed, are they? I try to clean myself off with my napkin, though I feel like I'm only managing to make a bigger mess of myself. I have managed to get sticky sauce everywhere.

"I'm going to the bathroom to clean my hands off … and maybe my face too. I'm sure that I have sauce all over my face." I stand and say to Josh, who is currently trying to wipe the mark off of his tie.

"Oh, what? Did you get yourself covered in sweet and sour sauce? No, wait. That would be me!" I begin to laugh at his comment, I just can't help it. We both know that it was me who'd gotten the sauce on his tie. I was trying to encourage him to try one of the sticky prawns, but my aim was, well, let's just say that it wasn't exactly great.

The prawn slipped through my fingers, leaving a sticky trail down his chin, down his tie, and then finally ended up resting in his lap. The look he'd given me had been priceless, but I did the polite thing and offered to get it for him. The blush that crossed over his cheeks when I did make me feel bad for teasing him.

"And did I drop food down myself? No. Again that would have been you!" He says through laughter. I walk by him with a smile, and as I walk away, I can hear his deep sexy laugh following me through the air.

The toilets are very clean, and they're decorated beautifully. They're covered with orchids, which make them smell amazing. I make a mental note to find a florist and get more fresh flowers. I really do love the smell of fresh flowers. I could add them to the bouquet Josh gave to me.

As I leave the toilet and start making my way back down the hall, I only manage to reach about half way along when I feel some hands grabbing at me from behind, one covering my mouth while the other is gripping tightly around my waist. I am pulled into a dark side room, and I'm begin to panic but then something happens… I feel a flurry of butterflies flying through my stomach. My body seems to know who it is before my mind can wrap itself around what's happening. *It's Rocco.* It can only be him.

In the next instant, I'm turned around until my back is pressing hard up against the wall, and I find myself being pinned there by a large, hard body. He removes his hand from my mouth, and I gasp a sharp breath. My pulse has begun to race, and I need to try and calm myself down.

"Rocco? What the hell do you think you're doing?" I'm thankful that I'm able to keep my voice sounding strong and even. There's no evidence of the turmoil that's taking over my insides.

"How did you know it was me? And, more to the point, what are you doing here with him?" I swear I can hear a growl behind his words. I choose to ignore the first part of his question. I'm not going to openly admit to him the reaction my body has whenever he's close to me, especially when it's clear he doesn't want me in the same way.

"I'm here on a date. Not that it's really any of your business."

"Why him?" Is he being serious? I mean, what the hell? How dare he think that just because he doesn't want me that I'm not good enough for his friends, as well.

"Why him? It's him because he asked me, Rocco, and because he's a really nice guy." I can hear the anger building in my voice the more I speak. *Good.* Where does he get off treating me like this?

"I know he's a good guy, but I don't understand why you're with him." His voice becomes a little quieter, and he takes another breath.

"Rocco, you're making no sense whatsoever. I'm here on a date, so will you, please let go of me so I can get back to him?"

"No." Okay, I think I might actually start screaming soon, and I probably would have already if I wasn't making the most of the way Rocco's body is pressed up firmly against mine. The body contact I have with him now may never happen again, so I want to make the most of it and remember this moment.

"No? Oh my god, Rocco! What is wrong with you? I'm getting whiplash from all of your different mood swings. I get it, alright? You don't want me, so you think I'm not good enough for your friends either. Well, you'll just have to get over it because I happen to like Josh, and I think that he likes me too." I feel tears brimming in my eyes and try hard not to blink so they won't fall. The last thing I want to do is cry. He doesn't need to know how much he's hurting me.

"Is that honestly what you think, Makenzie? You seriously think that I don't want you?"

"What the hell am I supposed to think? You invited me out for the night, but the experience of dancing with me made you run away, and not only run, you disappeared for a week! You didn't even go to your training! You really must have been embarrassed about dancing with me if you felt you needed to

69

leave your life because of it!" The frustration I'm feeling becomes evident in my voice, and it takes a lot of control not to shout the words at him.

"Makenzie." That's the only word I hear before his lips crash onto mine. I freeze in place, losing all thought from my mind apart from the words 'Oh my god'.

His lips are gentle at first, and he moves his tongue across my top lip, making my pulse race and my breath catch in my throat. My lip's part and I'm trying really hard to breathe. He uses this opportunity and tentatively slides his tongue into my mouth. He tastes of liquor, and all I want to do is suck his tongue. A moan escapes from my mouth when his tongue meets with mine. It's the only permission he needs to deepen the kiss. He presses his mouth harder against mine, and I feel his tongue reaching depths of my mouth that I don't think anyone has ever reached before.

He grinds his hips hard up against me, pushing me even harder against the wall. I can feel the evidence that the kiss is turning him on just as much as it is me. His arousal is rubbing me in such an amazing way that I can already feel my panties getting wet.

I slide my hands over his biceps and can feel how tight his muscles are as he continues to grip my body close to his. My hands make their way into his hair, where I take handfuls in-between my fingers and pull him even closer to me. I don't feel as though I could ever be close enough to him. His mouth is making love to mine, and I begin to move my hips in time with his tongue. I hook a leg up high around his hip, making my dress ride up my thigh. He skims his hand over the bare flesh of my inner thigh, sending a burning sensation to filter through my whole body.

I still can't believe how amazing it feels when he touches me. It feels like I've waited my entire life to be touched in this way. I'm not a virgin, far from it, but I honestly can't remember ever feeling this way before.

His hand moves higher, which in turn takes my dress higher and the moan I've been holding finally escapes into his mouth. With that, Rocco breaks the kiss. He places his forehead against mine gently and lowers my leg away from his waist. The only noise between us now is the sound of our breathing as we both gasp for breaths.

"Makenzie, I'm sorry." A look of remorse crosses into his eyes as he takes a step away from me.

"No! Don't you dare do this again! You don't get to do that, say that you're sorry and then just fucking disappear!" I look him straight in the eye, and feel myself pleading with him to not run away from me again.

When did I become the type of woman to beg a man?

"I can't do this … I shouldn't have kissed you, I'm sorry," I take a small step forward and place my forehead lightly onto his chest, trying to swallow back the tears I can feel brewing. I'm almost reaching breaking point. I don't understand. "You'll find yourself someone who'll be a lot better for you than I ever can be, Mackenzie." He says with sadness now lacing his voice.

"I'm a big girl, Rocco, I know what I want and I think that it's up to me to decide what I want in my life." I mumble into his chest, scared what I'll see if I look into his eyes. I feel him placing a soft kiss into my hair as he eases me away from him. When I'm able to hold my body upright on my own legs again, he backs away and then walks towards the doorway that leads back into the dining room.

"You look beautiful tonight, Makenzie, Josh is a very lucky man." As he mentions Josh's name, I notice his face flinching slightly. He turns back away and continues down the hall, but just as he's halfway through the door, he turns back to me and a small smile etches over the corner of his lips.

"I hope you enjoyed your coffee this week." With his parting comment, he walks completely through the door and out from my view.

Well, I'll be damned.

I return to the table and see Josh looking at me with a worried expression over his face. I must obviously look as bad as I'm feeling.

"Are you ok, Makenzie? You were away for a while, and you look a little flushed." I feel the heat rising into my cheeks again.

I sit back down in my seat and smile, ready to tell him that I'm fine but just as I'm about to, a giggle catches my attention. It sounds like one of those fake giggles that women make when they're flirting and trying to grab a guy's attention or something.

My eyes flick over to my left, and that's when I see it. The sight in front of me has the bile rising in my throat, and I can feel my stomach beginning to clench. I feel as though I want to be sick and have to try my hardest to stop myself from heaving.

Sitting at a table on the other side of the room is Rocco and Mason. Rocco is staring directly at me, but that isn't what catches my attention. My eyes land on the very beautiful brunette sitting beside him. She's draping herself over his arm. She has both of her arms wrapped around Rocco's and is gently rubbing her breasts up and down him while whispering something into his ear. I continue to watch her and then hear her letting out another loud giggle.

I can't believe that he's just given me a hard time about being here with Josh. And, more importantly, I can't believe that he just kissed me the way he did when all the time, he's here with someone else. Okay, I know that I'd kissed him back, but he's the one who made the first move, not me. It just goes to prove that it's only me that he's supposedly not good enough for. He doesn't seem to have any problems taking anyone else out.

"Makenzie?" I turn my gaze back to Josh, who's sitting with a confused look over his face now.

"I'm sorry. Listen, I'm sorry but I've a really bad headache coming on. Would you mind if we leave now? I think I need to get myself to bed and lie down."

"No, of course. No problem. Let me just go and settle up the bill and then I'll get you home." He smiles such a sweet, caring smile at me before he stands and leaves the table.

I feel like a total bitch. Josh has been nothing but incredibly sweet to me all night. I can't believe that I let Rocco kiss me when I came here with him Josh. Okay, let maybe isn't the right word, but I didn't exactly push him off me. No. *I pulled him closer.*

I stand when I see Josh heading back over to our table. He picks up my shawl from the back of the chair and gently places it around my shoulders. He keeps his arm around me and leads me towards the exit door.

Removing his arm from around my shoulders, he walks ahead of me and opens it up wide, lifting his hand up in front of us and gesturing for me to walk ahead of him. As I'm about to walk out into the street and cool, fresh air, I hear Mason speak. He says something that's unintelligible to me at first, but then raises his voice slightly and his words become more coherent. "Just leave it." I turn my head to the side and look over my right shoulder, seeing Mason is now standing right in front of Rocco, with his hands placed solidly on his chest. It's as though he's holding Rocco back.

I turn my attention back to Josh when I feel him placing his arm around my shoulders again, I smile up at him. He really is sweet.

Just as the door is about to close behind us, I hear an angry growl from inside the restaurant.

"Fuck!"

****

I wake up on Sunday morning, but feel as though I haven't slept at all. My head is feeling tight, and I pray to myself that I don't have a migraine coming on.

I spent the entire night tossing and turning. I just couldn't tear my thoughts away from thinking about Rocco. I'm so confused by him, his words and his actions, they never seem to match up.

His words seem to always push me away, but his actions just pull me back to him. It had felt as though he enjoyed the kiss as much as I had, but then he told me he was no good.

Ugh! I refuse to think about all of this again.

I jump out of my bed and grab a pair of jogging bottoms and tank top, not overly glamorous I know, but they're extremely comfortable. Today I plan to go out and explore the area. It has become obvious that I know very little about the place where I live, and an added bonus is that it's a beautiful day outside. I will walk and listen to music. Nothing more!

I tie my hair back in a lose ponytail and grab my phone and earphones from the kitchen table before making my way out of the door. My first stop of the day is the coffee shop so I can get some breakfast. A coffee and a donut. Is there any better way to start the day? I eat inside but order my coffee to go. With my earphones in and my favourite playlist playing, I head in the opposite direction than I usually go.

It doesn't seem to take long before I notice that I'm leaving the busy streets behind, and all I can see ahead of me is the green grass and trees instead. I had no idea that I've been living so close to such a beautiful area. It's a large open space, and granted its a little overgrown, but you can still make out little pathways that have been worn into the ground by the other people who have as walked this way.

I follow one of them through some trees. The shade is cool and most welcome. It's nice to have a break from the sun sometimes. I keep walking and eventually see a pond ahead of me. It's not huge or anything, but I decide to just stand and admire the scenery, watching the ducks as they swim around on it.

Over on the other side, there's a man out walking his dog, though the dog seems to be far more interested in chasing the ducks around than stretching its legs. I smile and think to myself that I must bring some bread with me the next time I come here so I can feed them.

I sit myself down on a small grassy hill beside the pond. It's so peaceful and relaxing here that it would be easy to stay for hours and just take in the amazing view, unlike the park, the only noise that I hear now is the splashing water from the water in front of me and birds as they sing.

My favourite song begins to play through my earphones, and I decide to lay back on the grass and listen to the words while staring up at the bright blue sky above. The songs about being broken and left in pain. I wonder if Rocco really is broken, and if he is, I wonder if it would ever be possible to fix him, make him complete again. Once the song has finished, I check the time and see that it's going on for almost four o'clock. I should start thinking about getting home. I make my way back up the path and follow the same trail I used when I came down here. I think it's most likely that I'll be visiting a lot more from now, especially when I want to be alone. But for now, I need to get home and get some laundry done.

I'm about to hit the steps that lead up to my apartment when I see something lying at the very top of them. As I reach the entrance doors, I see a single red rose lying on the ground. I pick it up and look for a name or card, but there isn't one.

Opening my door, I make my way inside and wonder who it's for, but then come to the conclusion that it must have been left there by mistake. I mean, who leaves a flower without so much as a card?

Placing it in a small vase on my kitchen windowsill, I smile before going in search for my dirty clothes. Once I've located them, and my arms are full, I'm just returning back through to the kitchen when I hear a knock on the front door.

Dropping the clothes in front of the washing machine, I make my way over to answer it and when I open it up, there's no one on the other side. *Strange*. Just as I'm about to close it back up again, I glance down and there, sitting on the top step is another single red rose.

I pick it up, inhale its scent and then walk down the stairs to follow whoever it was who left it here. If someone's leaving these at the wrong door then I should tell them. I look around, but there's no one in sight.

I go back up to my apartment and place the new rose with the other one in the vase. I love roses, so they're a very welcome addition to my kitchen.

Once I've put a load of clothes in the washing machine and after I've cleaned the bathroom, I'm returning back to the kitchen when there's yet another knock at the door. I move quicker this time to answer it. I really want to catch who is doing this, but again when I open it up, there's no one there. This time though there's a difference. Instead of a single rose sitting on the ground, there's what looks to be a dozen red roses. I pick them up and move back into the apartment, walking to place them on the kitchen table. My eyes land on the bouquet, and I notice that this time there is a card, and it has my name written on the front. My hands begin to shake as I take the card and open it.

There, on a simple white card, is one word written with an elegant scrawl.

'Sorry'

I hold the card close to my chest, finally realising who has been sending them. There's only one person who would feel the need to say sorry to me.

Rocco.

Before I can even stop myself from doing it, a huge smile spreads over my face. Oh, I really am in trouble.

No matter what he says to me, his actions are what I'm going to be reading from now on. And, what's more, these actions say that he wants to be something to me. Now, though, I've just got to figure out what.

Chapter Eight

I arrive to work with both a coffee in my hand, and a plan in my mind. I've decided that I need to have a talk with Rocco. I need to try and understand what's going on in that head of his because only then will I be able to work out what's going on in my own.

I walk behind the reception desk and place my bag into the staff drawer before locking it closed. I'm always getting here early these days because I like to take a walk through the building before I actually start my shift. I like to make sure the swimming team have everything they need.

As I'm walking through the spectator's area, I look over to watch the swimmers as they train. There are two swimmers, and they're standing at the side of the pool, chatting with each other.

I stop myself from walking any further when my eyes land on one of them. Well, it's not really him who catches my eye, it's the tattoo he has over his skin. Thick black patterns cover his back. They seem to start just below his swimming trunks and continue up his spine, disappearing over the right side of his shoulders. It looks like a tribal design to me, but I can't be sure. All I know is that it looks amazing. As he turns slightly, I can see that it continues over his shoulder and runs down his right arm. As I follow the pattern with my eyes, a feeling of recognition begins to stir. I'm almost one hundred percent sure that I've seen this tattoo before, or at least some of it. And that's when it hits me.

It's Rocco.

I recognise the tattoo from the night we went out to the club together. I haven't seen the rest before now because they're

78

usually all in the water when I do my regular morning walk through.

Almost as though he can feel my stare burning into his back, he turns around, and his eyes land directly on mine. We stare into each other's eyes, and I swear I lose the breath that was trying to leave my lungs when I notice the heat entering his eyes.

The guy next to him continues to speak, but then turns to see where Rocco is looking. *It's Josh*. He raises his hand and waves at me while throwing a smile. I return his wave with one of my own, and when I look back to Rocco, I see that he's masked his emotions again. His eyes are now guarded. He turns briefly speaks with Josh and then walks away from him. Okay, so I think that talking with him today may be harder than I'd originally thought.

I follow my usual route for my walk through, checking the towels in the men's changing area first and then making sure the steam room is all in full working order. I check the back doors to make sure they're locked, and then make my way to the function suites to make sure that they're clean and tidy.

I head back to the male changing rooms to make sure the swim team haven't used up all of the towels. The team usually take to the pool in two different shifts because there isn't enough room for them to all practice at one time. My return journey is usually well timed in between the two shifts when they switch over, and so I'm usually free to walk through without seeing anything that may traumatise me too badly.

As I walk by the showers, I can hear the sound of water running., I walk towards the shower room, thinking that one of the guys has left one of the showers on by mistake, making sure to mention it to them tomorrow so it won't happen again in the future.

As I turn the corner, there he is. He's standing under the running water with both hands placed against the tile wall. His head is dropped forward, and the water is hitting his shoulders and running down his back. I take a moment and watch as the water flows over his muscles and over his tattoo. His muscles appear tight, and I notice them flexing slightly when he moves some more until he's back under the spray. He is all carved muscle, there is not an inch of fat anywhere. I should walk away and leave him to his peace, but I just can't seem to be able to move. I need to keep watching him because I don't honestly think that I've ever seen anything quite as beautiful as him in this very moment. I'm so engrossed in watching that I don't even notice him turning the water off. Before I can move, he's already turned around and is looking directly at me.

"Oh … em … I'm sorry. I thought someone had left a shower on … I just came in to switch it off and …" He walks slowly towards me and reaches over my right shoulder, making my breath hitch. I feel stupid as soon as I realise that he's reaching behind me for a towel from the rack I'm standing in front of, and not for me. He roughly dries his hair before wrapping the towel around his waist. His hair is messy, and my fingers are itching to run through it again the memory of what it feels like in-between my fingers is still fresh in my mind.

"Is that all you were in here for?" He's standing so close to me now that I can feel the coolness from his chest working its way through my top. His shower doesn't seem to have done anything to heat his body back up after being in the cool water of the pool.

"No. I wanted to say thank you for the flowers, as well. And, to let you know that there was really no need to apologise to me." There's a reason to apologise, of course there is, but I couldn't just stay standing here, staring at him and saying nothing at all. I don't want to come across as a bitch when I want this to go well.

"I needed to say sorry, Mackenzie because I should never have kissed you."

"But, why, Rocco? I wanted you to kiss me, and if I'm to be completely truthful with you, I want you to kiss me again. So, why shouldn't you?" I ask in a soft voice. I'm feeling a little embarrassed asking, but I want to know why he thinks that what happened between us was a mistake.

He inhales a deep breath and closes his eyes firmly shut for a few moments. When he reopens them, all I can see inside them is pain. He looks … *broken*. My breath catches but it's for a completely different reason this time. I want to hold him. I want to take away the pain I can see washing over him away.

He lifts his hand and gently cups the side of my face, running a thumb over my cheek as he looks down to my lips. He shakes his head and says in a rough voice, a voice that sounds like he is holding so much emotion back.

"I'm no good for you, Makenzie. I can't give you anything, and you deserve everything. I'm broken. I'm not a complete man. I'm, I'm … useless." He whispers the last word and releases my cheek before walking away from me with his head hanging down low.

I feel a tiny piece of my heart beginning to break. I don't understand what he means. Broken and useless? How is that possible?

All I know is that the pain he just showed me is a deep pain. A pain that's tearing him apart inside. With tears burning my eyes, I return back to the reception desk and attempt to try and get on with what I'm being paid to do.

Rocco must have left while I wasn't at the reception desk. I didn't see him again at all after we spoke in the showers and now that I'm leaving work for the day, I know that he's avoiding me again. I need to find out what's happening because I can't leave things the way they are. Something is really wrong, and I want, no, I need to know what it is so I can decide if it's me or not.

I know that what I'm about to do is lame, but it's the only thing I can think to do, and so long as it works, I really don't care. I hold my cell to my ear as I sit down on the bench in the park, with my after work coffee in my other hand

"Hello?"

"Mason? Hi, it's Makenzie." I hold my breath, hoping that I haven't made a mistake calling him.

"Hi Makenzie. And to what do I owe this pleasure?" I can hear the smile in his voice and feel my shoulders beginning to relax.

"I was wondering if you could possibly meet with me? There's something that I want to chat with you about."

"Why is it that what you just said is starting to scare me a little?" He laughs down the phone at me.

"I swear it's nothing scary. It's just something you can maybe help me with. I'll even buy the coffee."

"Ok, but I'm busy just now. Could you give me maybe an hour?"

"Thanks, Mason. I'll meet you in the coffee shop just by the park. I'll grab us a table." I am thankful to him because maybe I'll be able to get some answers from him about Rocco, well, if Mason is willing to share them with me.

"No worries. I'll see you then." We say our goodbyes and then I press the end button on my mobile. I stay in the park for a little while longer, having decided that's it's not worth my while going home.

I see Mason before he notices me, so I wave over to him to catch his attention. He smiles when he sees me, and I have to admit that if I wasn't falling hard for Rocco, then I'd most likely be trying to get his attention.

These thought are actually starting to shock me. I'm falling for Rocco? It's the first time I've admitted even to myself that I really do have feelings for him. Arriving at the table, Mason pulls me right out from my thoughts as he sits down heavily on the chair across from me.

"You will not even believe the day I've had. I was so glad when you called, so I had an excuse to leave." He states without even so much as a hello.

"Well, I'm glad. *I think*." I say to him with a smile.

"I'll try to take what you just said as a compliment. I didn't know what you prefer to drink, so I waited until you got here to order for you."

"Yes, it was a compliment so stop fishing, and there's no need to worry about that, I'll be back in a minute, I'll just go and grab a coffee." He winks as he stands up from the table, before walking towards the counter to place his order.

Seriously? Do these guys take lessons on how to be, so God damn charming? He's as bad as Rocco with his charm … and, there we go again. Back to Rocco. I can't manage to get the guy out of my mind for more than five minutes at a time these days, and if I don't stop soon then it's going to make me go bloody insane.

Returning to the table and placing his coffee down in front of him, Mason begins, "I so need this … Rocco has been walking around as though someone kicked his damn puppy. I've seen the man in a bad mood before, don't get me wrong, but not anything as close to this in a very long time." Well, if I was waiting for a way to start a conversation about Rocco, here it is. I look down at the cup in my hand and try to avoid looking directly at Mason when I speak. "Rocco is the reason I asked you to meet with me. I'm sorry. I hope you don't mind."

"Okay, well, that sure explains it." My gaze shoots up to meet his and I see that he's watching me while a grin forms over his mouth. He looks as though what I just said to him has explained all the questions and the answers of the universe to him.

"What? What does it explain?"

"That man has been having a pretty hard time ever since you came into his life. Before he was just going about his life, living it like he has gotten used to things again, but then one day, he arrives at work with a smile. An actual real smile. I don't want to tell you how long it's been since I've seen one of those over Rocco's face. But, since the day he met you, he's been tied in knots." He's been tied in knots? I'm the one who doesn't know what's happening between us, but he's the one who has been tied up in knots?

One step forward and two steps back.

"Then why does he keep pushing me away? I know I shouldn't be asking you, and I'm sorry for being unfair, but he won't talk to me. He confuses me with the things he says and then avoids me right afterwards." A sad look washes over Mason's features.

"He doesn't mean to, he just doesn't know what to do or how to cope." He answers with a softer voice now as he shrugs his shoulders.

"Ugh! Do you both take classes in talking in riddles?" I know I shouldn't be getting frustrated with Mason, but I'm getting no further forward with him than I would with Rocco. Mason laughs though it sounds like a sad laugh. I feel my stomach drop, knowing that I'm missing something here. *Something big.*

"Like I've said before, Mackenzie. This isn't my story to tell. It needs to come from Rocco, if or when he's ready to tell you, he will."

"Please help me, Mason?" I know I'm beginning to sound desperate now, but at this moment, I really would be willing to get down on my knees and beg if it meant he would help me understand.

"I like him, Mason. I *really* like him, and I don't want him to keep running away from me all the time. I just … I need to know if he likes me too, or if I'm seeing something between us that isn't there."

"He likes you, Makenzie, like *really* likes you. But, there is something holding him back. It's been so long since he's felt anything for anyone that he isn't sure what to do with his feelings. All I can say is that he's been hurt in the past. Hurt so badly and to the point where I wasn't so sure if he'd ever find himself again or not." Masson's voice has taken on such a serious tone that all I can do is sit looking at him. There's a part of me that doesn't want to hear any of this, but I know that I have to listen.

"Look, he was in an accident … and, well, we almost lost him, but he fought to stay. He's the strongest guy I know, but while he fought to build his body again, I saw his spirit break. His ex, Elle? She is a complete bitch, but, again, that's his story. I've said too much already. Know it's not you, and if you really want my advice, then here it is. If I were you, I'd push him to open up before he pushes you away completely." And with those last few words, I at last feel some hope building inside me. Mason thinks I have a chance so long as I don't let Rocco push me away. I just need to decide if I think he's worth the fight. With a smile forming on my lips, I already know the answer. Yes. He's totally worth fighting for.

Chapter Nine

The past few days have flown by so quickly. Work has been busier than usual where the schools have broken up for the holidays. I've finally been paid, and after I did a little happy dance, I decided to paint my bedroom when I wasn't in work. It is taking a while to get done around my work hours, but I don't care, I am having fun and that's all I care about. The only thing that I'm not so happy with is that I haven't seen Rocco since our chat, but Josh did mention that he is away on a business trip. While painting I have had plenty of time to think how I am going to deal with this thing between us and I have decided I am going to pursue him, take the role of chaser for a change. I refuse to let him slip away without seeing if it will go anywhere.

I had sent Mason a text to thank him for his chat and to ask for Rocco's cell number. He was more than happy to give me it. I think he just wants to see Rocco happy, and he thinks he will be with me, and so started my plan to get the man I want. I sent him a message this morning asking him how he was. I haven't heard anything back but to be honest I didn't expect him to reply just yet, I just wanted him to know I was thinking about him.

So at this moment I am wearing tracksuit bottoms that I have turned into painting shorts by cutting the legs off, a T-shirt I found that must have belonged to Carl since it's far too big, and I have had to tie it in the back. While looking like a hot mess, I'm dancing around my room to cheesy 80s music, and I think I am wearing more of the hot pink paint that I have chosen, than I have on the walls. I never claimed to be a good painter, but I'm having fun and to me that's the most important thing. For the first time in a very long time I feel happy, I feel like my life may be going in the right direction. I have my own place, a job that I really enjoy and a guy I like...I just need to get him now. As I am singing at the top of my voice, I hear a knock on my door. I hope it's not my neighbours coming to complain, let's just say that my singing is worse than my painting. I open the door, and I nearly drop my paintbrush when I see who is standing there, looking so sexy in jeans and a simple black T-shirt. Rocco.

"Hi." I manage, even though my mouth has suddenly gone very dry. I see his eyes move down my body. I suddenly remember what I'm wearing, or should that be how little I'm wearing, and I feel a blush move up my face.

"Hi." He says as his eyes work their way up my body, and I swear I can see the heat in them, or at least I hope I do. I'm not even sure how long we stand there and just look at each other, it could have been minutes or it could have been days.

"You're dripping on the floor." He says, and I watch as a smile creeps up at the sides of that sexy mouth of his.

"What? Oh God!" I scream and notice that I'm dripping paint all over the floor from the paintbrush that's still in my hand. I turn around and hurry back towards my bedroom practically covered in paint. I can hear Rocco letting out a bellowing laugh from behind me.

"Come in!" I shout while trying to clean up as much of the paint from my hand as possible.

"I'll be right out, I'm just going to try and clean myself up a little bit."

"Do you have any cloths, and something to clean with? I will get this paint before it dries."

"Yes. Under the sink in the kitchen, there are old cloths and detergent. Thank you." I make my way over to the bathroom to wash my hands, and to try and compose myself from the shock of him being here. Calm down, you wrote him a message. You wanted him to think about you, well he's definitely thinking about you, he's just thinking about you as he cleans the paint from your hall floor. I dry my hands while checking myself out in the mirror, I cringe when I see my reflection. I look horrible, I have paint in my hair and on my face but short of having a shower there isn't much that can be done about it. I make my way back out towards the living room to find him on his knees cleaning the spots of paint I left as I ran.

"I'll get the rest. Be careful not to get any on you, I can't afford to replace your jeans." I meant it as a joke, but it came out sounding very serious. I would have been subtler if I had just told him I couldn't afford expensive clothes like he can.

"Don't worry. That's it all finished now." He stands up and brushes his hands down the front of his jeans.

"And look, no paint." He gives me that smile that I love, the one that scrunches his eyes up and makes me melt just a little. Ok, it makes me melt a lot. I take the cloth from him and walk towards the kitchen to rinse it in the sink. He follows behind me and leans against the doorframe.

"Not that I'm not happy that you are here, but can I ask why you are here?" I busy myself with rinsing the cloth so I don't have to look at him. I am still trying to calm my nerves, he makes my body go out of control when he is near, and being inside my apartment is very near.

"Honestly? I don't know why I'm here. I got your message this morning on the way home from a meeting, and I just wanted to see you. So when I got in my car to drive home I just kinda found myself parked outside your door." I don't think he realises how much he just made my heart stutter, he wanted to see me? That has to be good. Drying my hands I turn to face him again, but I still can't bring myself to look at his face, to show him the hope in my eyes.

"Do you want a coffee? Or a tea with no sugar?" I can't help but tease him, and I know he knows I am just teasing when he laughs.

"Yeah, a tea with no sugar would be great."

We have moved, and we are both now sitting on the couch in the living room, me with my coffee and as I guessed, Rocco with his tea. I have my feet tucked under me sitting sideways so I can look at him as we speak. He is sitting right next to me, almost close enough to touch, he has one leg crossed over the other knee. I have never really paid much attention to his legs, or anything below his butt if I'm totally honest, but his thighs look powerful with his muscles bunched up. They make his jeans stretch tight over them, and it makes my mind wander a little about how much power he has in them. He is looking down at his cup, and the silence is stretching between us, I know I need to make the first move here, make him feel comfortable around me.

"So, how did you get onto the swimming team?" This topic seemed like a safe place to start but going by the look that has appeared on his face I can see that I have made a mistake. He keeps his head down avoiding my eyes as he answers me.

"I was in a pretty bad motorbike accident a few years back, I needed something to help with rehab and it was the thing that was easiest on my body at the time." He turns to look at me, and I am sure the look of pain in his eyes must match the look of shock in mine. I reach my hand over and place it on his thigh; I just can't help but try to give him comfort. He looks down at my hand, I wonder if I should move it but I decide not to. I am so surprised with his answer I don't even notice the muscles of his leg clenching under my hand...ok I noticed just a little.

"Oh my God Rocco. I'm sorry I had no idea. Was it bad? No sorry...look you don't need to answer that." I shake my head, I can't believe that I actually just asked him that. I mean I can see he is feeling awkward by the question and the best I can come up with is to ask him more about it.

"No, its ok. I don't mind telling you about it, it's just been a long time since someone hasn't known the story. It was pretty big news around here. You know, motorbike accident leaves young man fighting for life in a coma." He gives a little snort and then turns back to look at me. I'm not sure what emotion is showing on my face, but I know what I'm feeling inside. Coma? Fighting for life? Shock and horror are my two main emotions at the moment.

"Oh no, Makenzie. I'm sorry, I shouldn't have just blurted it out like that. Look you can see I'm fine now, it all turned out ok." He uses his hands to indicate to his body, but I just stare at him, I will the words in my head to come out my mouth in some sort of coherent order.

"A coma? Seriously Rocco...a coma?" Ok, that was a pretty good attempt at a sentence. I just need to try and calm all the emotions that are running through me, if I can get myself to calm down slightly. He's right, I am getting worked up and he is sitting in front of me proof that he survived.

"Yeah, a coma. I was on a coma for 8 days." The more he tells me about it, the more my heart races. I know he's fine, the proof is sitting on my couch right now, but knowing this had happened to him is breaking my heart. He has been through so much, but you would never know.

"What happened?"

"I really don't remember much of the accident. I remember being out on my motorbike, I loved that thing," He has a smile on his face as he mentions his bike, even after everything he has been through he is still like a big kid talking about his toy.

"It was a nice dry day and I was out for what I called 'a head clearing ride'. I had just had an argument with Elle, that was my girlfriend at the time, and I needed to get away. I had just hit the motorway, and I was opening the bike up a bit, I needed to just let go. That was the last thing I remember until I woke up in the hospital eight days later."

"Did you find out what happened? I mean, do you know what caused the accident?" My voice comes out as barely a whisper, but he obviously hears me as he answers.

"I was told after I woke up, they had done some big investigation into what had happened. They told me I was overtaking a truck when one of its tires blew out, it lost control and hit me. In that fight, I came off worst. The truck driver walked away, and it took me over a month to walk again."

"You couldn't walk?" I almost screech. I hadn't seen the conversation going this way. I think I would have been less surprised if he had told me he used to be a woman. I feel like all I am doing is sitting dumbly listening then repeating things he is saying. I just don't know what to say to him. What do you say to someone who has been to hell and survived?

"When I woke up, they had already done three operations on my spine and one on my brain. The one on my brain was just to relieve pressure, thankfully I had been wearing a helmet or I probably wouldn't be sitting here now. The pressure had affected my brain though, and I found it hard to speak and it was very slow for a long time. I remember Mason saying he loved it, he finally got the last word in an argument." This time his words make me smile, I could totally picture Mason making light of the situation, needing to make Rocco feel better. I know they had been friends for a long time, and I know it would have hurt him to watch Rocco go through everything he did.

"Did it happen often, even then?" I ask making him laugh.

"Not really. I still won the arguments; they just took a bit longer. The feeling in my legs took longer to come back than my speech. They weren't sure if it ever would, but I was determined I wasn't going to be stuck in a chair for the rest of my life. If there was even a small chance that I would walk again, I was going to fight. After a while, I got some feeling back, and after another few weeks of rehab I managed to finally stand. I needed something to build up my strength without putting too much pressure on my spine…so that's how the swimming came about. I didn't expect to fall in love with it so much though, and I suppose you know the rest of the story." I just can believe what he has just told me, the story is like something from an afternoon special. What his body has been through, and there is no evidence of it, he has no scars that I can see, no limps, nothing to show the journey he has been on.

"Oh my god Rocco. I just don't know what to say to you. What you have been through. You are the bravest person I know." His face clouds over and he looks away from me.

"I'm not brave. I put a lot of people through hell with my accident, I mean no one should have had to deal with that." I'm sitting looking at him in complete confusion. I'm not sure where he got the idea that he isn't brave. I don't think I could have gone through what he did and still have the energy to fight to get better. He is the poster child for brave.

"Rocco what are you talking about? You must have been brave to work so hard and overcome everything you did. Why don't you see that?"

"No! The people around me were brave. They had no option but to help me, and it was all my fault. All I was a burden to

93

them. " Now I'm even more confused and I'm getting lost in this conversation. The words that are coming our his mouth don't connect to the story that he has just told me, and I have no idea why he would think any of these things. Someone has put some really strange ideas into his head about his accident and the impact it had on people. His head is dropped onto his chest and he is obviously trying to avoid looking at me. I reach over and gently lift his chin up until he is looking me in the eyes.

"I don't know who told you that you were a burden Rocco, but I can tell you sitting here listening to your story that I admire you. You came back fighting from something that you didn't ask for, and it could have ended your life." His eyes have started to look glassy with a build-up of tears that he's trying not to let fall, and I know if he starts crying I'm going to follow with own tears. Something is tearing Rocco up inside, and I want to know what, there is a darkness there that doesn't need to be. He needs someone to build him up after being torn down, and I want to be the person to help him.

"Who told you these things? Who made you feel like this?" He is still staring into my eyes, and I can see the indecision flash across his face, he is trying to decide if he is going to let me in. I move closer to him on the couch, I place one foot on the floor and my bent leg is now tight against his thigh. I can't get any closer to him without sitting on his lap. I feel the heat of his leg against my bare skin, but I can't let it affect me. This isn't the time to let my racing hormones take control, this is the time for me to give my support to the man that I want to know more about. I need to know who has caused this pain that is haunting him. I know he isn't going to answer me, so I gently place my hand on his chest as I ask again,

"Rocco, please. Tell me who told you this?" He closes his eyes and takes a deep breath as my hand makes contact with him. His hand comes up and rests on top of mine on his chest, his fingers work their way in between mine and he grasps them tightly. His head drops again, and he rests his mouth on top of our joined fingers.

"Rocco?"

"Elle." One simple word whispered. That was all he says, but I can see the pain it causes to say it. My heart shatter's for him. How could someone you love make you feel like that? I can't speak, I don't know what to say so I do the only thing I can think of. I climb onto him and straddle his lap. I put my arms around his neck and hold him, and in my mind I know I never want to let go. It takes a few moments but I soon feel Rocco's arms working their way around my waist, he holds me so tight and places his face into the crook of my neck. I just hold him, trying to show him how I feel about him. It's the closest we have been since the kiss, but I know that neither of us is feeling the sexual tension that is usually there, this is all about comfort and need of another kind.

I'm not sure how long we sit there holding each other, but he never eases his hold around me. I can still feel his breath on my neck, where his mouth is gently placed against it. I am trying not to be affected by his closeness, the last thing he needs at this moment is for me to get turned on, but the longer I am in his arms, the harder it is not to feel his body pushing against me. His hands on the bare skin of my waist, the way his breath is creating heat on my neck. I find myself running my hands up the back of his neck and through his hair. I feel unaware of what I'm doing, and my hands seem to have a mind of their own. When I feel his body tense underneath mine, and I realise I've made a big mistake. I start to pull away from him, but his arms tighten even more around me making me relax back into his hold. I am trying desperately to calm my erratic breathing before I make a total fool of myself, but he really doesn't help me when I feel his lips make full contact with my neck. I think that my heart is about to beat out of my chest, and I am convincing myself that it was an accident when they make contact again, this time with a little more pressure making it obvious that he is meaning to do it. His lip's part as he kisses my neck again, and I feel his warm tongue flick out to taste me. My breath catches in my throat and I have to remind myself to start to breath. Rocco's lips gently move up my throat towards my jaw while one of his hands move up to the back of my head and gently grabs my hair, pulling my head back to give him better access. The pressure he has on my hair is bordering on pain, but all I feel is pleasure. I can't stop the moan that leaves me as his mouth makes contact with that sensitive spot behind ear, I also can't stop my hips that automatically grind onto his lap. It's now his turn to let out a groan. Goosebumps instantly appear all over my body, how can a man have such an effect on me? I was with Carl for three years, and I never had this reaction to him, not even at the beginning. I was so focused on the feeling of him under my body that I start a little when he speaks into my ear.

"I want to kiss you Makenzie. It's all I ever think about, the taste of you on my tongue. I can still remember it from our last kiss, you are the sweetest thing I have ever tasted. I need more, so I am going to kiss you now.....but I can't be with you." My breathing has gone erratic at the words breathed into my ear. I want to give him everything he needs, but I also want to give him more so I need to ask him,

"You don't want to be with me?"

"No Makenzie. I want to be with you, I said I can't be with you." All thought of asking him to clarify what he means flees from my mind when his lips crashed down onto mine. Gone is the gentleness of his lips from before, this kiss is claiming, he is taking what he wants from me but I am more than willing to give it all to him. I move my hands from around his neck and run them down his chest, feeling the contours of his abs through his shirt. He is hard and defined, his body is every woman dream. I release another involuntary moan into his mouth as I continue my exploration of his body. The hand that he still has on my waist grips harder, hard enough that I am sure there will be a bruise left tomorrow, and he pulls me closer so that we are now chest to chest. I can feel the hardness of his erection pushing up into me where I sit, with only my little shorts and his jeans between us there is no way to hide how excited he is, also how big he is. Part of my mind starts wishing that our clothes would magically vanish, but that thought…or any thought really doesn't last long as his hand slips inside my T-shirt and up over my ribs. Rocco's lips pull away from mine, and he touches his forehead to mine, we are both breathing hard now, his fingers are still rubbing a pattern just below the underside of my breast, and I'm willing him to move his hand up. I want to feel his hands on me, my nipples have already gone hard in anticipation of his touch. I am just about to physically move his hand up onto my breast when his phone starts to ring. He lets out a long stuttered breath before reaching under my leg to retrieve the phone from his pocket.

"Hello." He listens to the person on the other side of the phone, but his eyes never leave mine.

"Can't you deal with it yourself Mason? I haven't even been home yet." I don't want to be nosey and listen to his call, but his hand has moved back to waist and is holding me on his lap. His lap where I can still feel the evidence of his arousal, I try to be good, but I just can't help myself now that I know its Mason on the phone. I push my knees out, so I sit further into his lap, pushing against his erection. His eyes roll into the back into his head, and he growls slightly in his throat. The phone drops slightly away from his ear, and I can hear Mason shouting through the earpiece.

"Rocco. Rocco man, where are you? I need to you to come to the garage ASAP. Rocco! Rocco are you there?" Opening his eyes Rocco looks at me with a small smile playing at the side of his mouth, and oh how I love that look on his face.

"Yeah Mason, I'm here. I'm on my way. No, I told you I'm not at home. No. No. I am just not at home just now, ok? I will see you soon…bye Mason." I can still hear Mason talking as Rocco presses the end call button, he puts his phone back into his pocket and reaches his hand up to hold my jaw. Running his fingers across my lips he says quietly,

"I'm sorry. I need to go, there is a problem at the garage and Mason says he can't handle it himself." Even though he is saying the words, he is making no effort to move away from me. I open my lips slightly and suck his thumb into my mouth as he tries to run it over them again.

"I swear Makenzie, if you keep doing things like that I won't be able to walk never mind move." He pulls his thumb from my mouth and with both hands on my waist he lift me from his lap and onto the couch next to him. He rises quickly before I can say anything, he runs his hands down the legs of his jeans trying to remove the creases on them and then readjusts himself as discreetly as he can. Turning he holds his hand out to me, and when I place my hand in his he pulls me from the couch.

"Thank you for the tea." He says as he walks towards the front door.

"You're very welcome," I say with a huge grin on my face.

"If you ever feel like another one, just text me." Rocco lets out a small laugh before placing a gentle kiss on my cheek.

"I'll call you soon." I watch him as he makes his way down the stairs, once he has turned the corner I close the door, leaning back on it I slide down until I am sitting on the floor. With a smile on my face I think about how well that had gone, not only did he kiss me again, he kissed me and didn't run away afterwards. As much as I would love to sit on the floor all day and think about how it felt to have Rocco's lips and hands on me, it was time to get this painting finished.

Chapter Ten

I arrived to work the next morning and was greeted with a single red rose sitting on the top of my desk. There was no card attached, but I knew instantly who it was from.

I'm getting so used to him not signing anything. He never seems to be able to admit that he likes to do sweet things.

I'm now sitting here, three days later with the same silly grin over my face as I had that day. I just can't seem to stop smiling, and even Matt has noticed. He first thought that I'd won the lottery or something, but the thing is I truly feel like I have.

Rocco and I haven't spoken since we kissed, but we have been messaging each other, and every day when he leaves the pool, I'm rewarded with a huge smile from him that truly melts my heart.

Every. Single. Time.

I know how closed off he is, so the fact that he's still texting me is a massive step forward for him. He isn't shutting me out this time, and I know that he's trying to give me at least some small part of him. I'm happy to get just a little piece of him at a time.

I notice the time on my computer and realise that I'm way behind on my shift already. I think that I've just spent the past ten minutes sitting here and daydreaming about him. Giving myself a mental telling off, I complete the start of the shift checks on the computer and then take a last sip of my coffee.

I next make my way over to check out the changing rooms and upstairs areas. The changing rooms look fine, and each of the racks are still filled high with towels, obviously no one has needed to use any since they were refilled on the last shift. I make my way through to the spectator's area so I can reach the back steps that lead to the functions areas above.

My eyes land on Rocco and see that he's standing by the pool, talking to Josh. I stop for a moment so I can just take him in. Yes, I understand how creepy this must sound, but I can't help but look at him. I notice that his body is tensed up, and his eyes are extremely dark. He doesn't look happy at all.

I'm just about to walk away and leave them to it, but then I see Josh lifting his hand up and beginning to point right into Rocco's face. I stay where I am and wonder what's going on.

I'm not sure what to do. If it's something to do with the swim team then it's really none of my business and I should leave them to it, but if it's the start of something else then I may need to go over and step in. There's no way I can have them fighting here.

As he continues to speak with Josh, I notice his eyes narrowing with what appears to be pure anger. He turns noticing that I'm standing here and watching them. His stance begins to relax slightly when his eyes land on mine, but it's not hard to see that he still isn't fully relaxed.

Josh turns around, and he is also now looking directly at me. The look he's throwing me seems to be one of hurt, though he quickly recovers and I see anger crossing over his entire features before he turns back towards Rocco.

I'm beginning to wonder what the hell's going on between the two of them. They've always appeared to be such good friends. I then see Josh lifting his hand and pointing into Rocco's face again, and now I know that I'm going to have to go in there and see what's going on. I can't just leave and walk away now I know this is happening.

The other guys are standing around them, though no one seems to be moving to step in between the two of them. They seem happy enough to stand around and watch as the two of them go at it. I'm going to have to go in there and do something.

Approaching them, I feel my heart beginning to race, almost out of control and my breaths are doubling their speed. I haven't been this close to a pool since the accident all of those years ago.

Actually, that's a lie. There has only been one other time, though it hadn't ended very well. I was with some friends at a pool party when we were in college, and some of the guys thought that it would be funny to throw some of the girls into the pool while still fully clothed.

I'd tried to escape through the crowd, but I only managed to draw more attention to myself because the next thing I knew, I was thrown over one of the guy's shoulders and he was stalking towards the pool.

I completely freaked out. I remember that I'd been screaming as though someone was murdering me and kept scratching at the guy's naked back. The pool area had gone completely quiet when I started to shout, and the guy quickly dropped me to my feet, but I couldn't hold myself up and ended up collapsed onto the ground and curled up into the foetal position.

I remember how scared I'd felt. I was so scared that I truly thought my heart was going to stop. As all the memories flood back into my mind, I feel the sweat beginning to form over my neck and back.

I haven't told Matt about my fear of the water, and thankfully he hadn't taken me in there during my interview.

I look up and see that Rocco and Josh are standing much closer to each other now. As I near, I can hear them shouting, even through the glass divide. I'll just have to do it. I have to go in there. If I could just get my body to move forward then I would go and intervene somehow.

I inhale a deep breath, urging myself to put my big girl panties on. I can do this. It's not as though I'm going in the water. I'll only be standing beside it. I move slowly across the room and push open the dividing door. Trying to stay calm, and walking as far away from the pool as I possibly can, I begin to approach them.

"Is everything ok, guys?" I know it's far from okay, but I thought that maybe this approach would calm them down a little bit.

"Yeah, everything's fine, Makenzie. There was just a slight disagreement, but it's all sorted now." Rocco turns in my direction and smiles at me. I notice that Josh still doesn't look happy, though. He moves closer to me before almost shouting in my face.

"Tell me, Makenzie. Are you going to be going out with me again? Because I thought that we'd had a pretty great night." I glance at Josh as he speaks, but I have no idea what to say. We did have a great time together, but I don't think that it would be fair to go out with him again. Especially because all I want and think about is Rocco.

"Um … well … yeah. We had a good time."

"That wasn't the question! Are you going to go out with me again?" His voice is almost demanding now and I can see him clenching his jaw firmly together, while grinding the words out through his teeth,

"Josh, leave it there. Don't take your bad mood with me out on Makenzie. Be a man and deal with me." I had never heard Rocco sound so angry in all the time I had known him, I'm shocked and I'm really not sure how to answer now.

"I am asking a simple question. She either wants to see me again, or she doesn't! This has nothing to do with you Rocco. Nothing!" I need to say something here, but I'm standing opened mouthed and in complete shock watching this unfold between the guys.

"I ...uh...I," It's all I manage to get out but I find myself moving closer to Rocco, putting more distance between me and Josh. He always seems like a nice guy, but I don't know him and he is really angry with me at the moment. I'm not sure where the anger is coming from, we have only been out the once, and even though it was fun there was nothing more.

"Please answer me Makenzie. I asked you, will you be going out on another date with me?" His voice is getting louder, and the other guys are still standing about watching us having our...discussion.

"Josh, I had a great time, and you are such a great guy, but I don't think I will be able to go out with you again." I'm so happy I finally manage to get a full sentence out and the fact that my voice sounds strong while I speak is an added bonus.

"Why not?" Josh's voice had quietened a lot, but I could still see the darkness in his eyes and I was actually a little scared of him. From the corner of my eye I can see Rocco moving towards me, I am now standing a little behind him, so I don't have the full force of Josh's glare straight on me.

"Look, Josh, you know why she won't go out with you again. I told you that I was interested in her, and I want you to step back, this is on me, not Makenzie. So if you want to be angry at someone be angry at me, I'm the dick in this equation." Rocco told Josh he was interested in me? It's strange that even in this situation that his words make me tingle.

"I'm not blaming her Rocco, I'm putting this fully on you. I thought we were friends, and you move in on the girl I like, I

104

thought you were a better guy than that." I have a funny thought run through my head while these two guys go at it. Even in this awkward situation I feel like we are in high school with the guys fighting over a girl.

"If we are putting it like that, you moved in on my girl. Everyone knew that I liked her, but no one took it seriously because it's me. Well, I'm sorry but this time I am going to fight for what I want."

"You are such a dick!" Josh growls at Rocco through clenched teeth, he reaches out and pushes Rocco on the chest with enough strength that it makes him take a step back. As Rocco moves back, he catches me on the chest making me stumble. The first of me realising that things aren't going to end well is when my foot goes out behind me, and I can't feel the ground. While we have been arguing, and I made my way behind Rocco, I have been getting closer to the edge of the pool without realising it. Now I'm fully aware of what is about to happen, and I can't do anything to stop it.

I feel my body tip back as I wave my arms trying to find something, anything to grab onto to stop the inevitable from happening. I slam into the water back first, and I feel my breath leaving my lungs in a painful gush from the force of the hit. I sink quickly, my panicked movements making no difference at all. I open my mouth to scream, realising instantly what a stupid thing it is to do, the water rushes into my mouth hitting the back of my throat before I even think to close my mouth again. I am sinking fast, and I watch as the light at the top of the pool get further away. I try not to panic, thinking if I relax I might float to the top of the pool again, but feel the bottom of the pool on my back as I look up through the water. I can see the top of the pool, but I can't control my body enough to get up there.

There was a time I could swim, and I try to remember what to do but the only visions in my head are of my baby sister, how she looked on the bottom of the pool that day many years ago. Her pale face as lay there with the life drained out of her. I was the big sister, I should have tried to do something to save her. My thoughts are crowding my head, and I try to focus, but it is so hard to do. I try to make my body work, make it do anything. The water is blocking my throat. I need to breathe. I am suffocating. I want to escape. I don't want to die, especially not this way. There is a darkness making its way into the edge of my vision, I try to blink it away but it is only getting larger. My lungs are burning, and I feel like my chest will explode. The blackness has nearly blocked my vision. I can't feel anything anymore. I'm numb. Just as the blackness takes over everything I feel an arm going around my waist and a chest pushing into my back. It's the last thing I remember.

Chapter Eleven

Everything hurts. My throat is killing me. Every time I try to swallow its feels as though I have razor blades sticking into my throat. I'm even finding it sore to breath. My lungs feel like there's someone sitting on my chest, and my ribs, yeah they're definitely sitting on my ribs, as well. I want to open my eyes, but when I try, they feel as though they're glued tightly shut. I try to turn my head, but wince and let out an involuntary moan, though it sounds more like a rasp by the time it makes its way out from my mouth.

"Makenzie?" I hear a buzzing sound beside me and turn away from the noise, hoping that my head isn't about to explode.

"Makenzie? Can you hear me?" I immediately recognise the soft spoken words. It sounds like Rocco, but I'm not entirely sure why he's here. Actually, now that I think about it, I'm not completely sure where here is. I try again to open my eyes and this time manage to a little, but the harsh white light that means through my eyelids has me instantly closing them again.

"Hey! Hey, she's moving! She hasn't spoken yet, but I think she's starting to wake up!"

Is Rocco talking to me? If he is then I really don't understand what he's talking about. My head is so fuzzy. It feels like I have the worst hangover ever imaginable, but I don't even remember having had a drink. I try to remember where I was and what I was doing, but I really can't think through the fog that's clouding my thoughts.

"Hi, honey. How are you feeling?" I hear a female voice that I don't think I recognise and then feel hands lightly touching my wrists, before something is stuck in my ear. I turn my head away quickly, but immediately wish that I hadn't.

"Its ok, hon. I'm only taking your temperature. It won't hurt you, I promise."

Temperature? Why is she taking my temperature? Where am I?

I force my eyes open again, even against the glare of the bright white lights. After blinking a few times, my eyes feel a little less grainy and I'm finally able to focus on my surroundings. The walls are white and look very sterile. There's a curtain pulled across on the right side of me, and behind it I can see a large window, though all it's displaying is the darkness outside. When I look down, I see that my legs are covered with a pale pink blanket and I'm wearing a hospital gown. *Hospital?* I turn my head to the left and see Rocco standing right beside my bed with a worried look over his face. His looks frighteningly pale, and his eyes are surrounded with dark circles.

"So, you've finally decided to wake up, have you?"

"W-w-what?" I manage to croak out. My throat is burning, and I'm finding it so hard to talk.

"She'll probably need a drink. I bet her throat is sore after everything she's been through. Would you like a drink, sweetie?" I don't think I've ever been called so many pet names as much as this before. I look over to the older nurse, fractionally nodding my answer. I try not to speak again, at least until I've had a drink. Rocco pours some water into a glass from the jug that's beside my bed on the night table, before placing a straw inside. He holds the straw against my lips, and I greedily drink as much as I possibly can.

"A little at a time. Just take little sips." I cough slightly, and I receive a knowing look from the nurse.

"My name is Elizabeth and I'm the night shift nurse. The doctor will be here soon to check on you. Do you remember anything about how you got here?" I shake my head, looking towards Rocco to see if he'll enlighten me. He looks at me with sympathetic eyes, but it's clear that he isn't going to tell me anything. He lifts the glass up to my lips again. I have another sip as the door to the room swings open, and when I turn to look, I see a tall, thin man wearing a white coat entering the room. He's wearing scrubs under his coat and carrying a patient file in his right hand.

"Makenzie? I'm Doctor Noelle. I was the A&E duty doctor when the ambulance first brought you in." He must see my eyes widen when he offers me this information. I have absolutely no idea what anyone's talking about.

"Do you know what happened or why you're here?" I feel like a mute and shake my head again. I can't seem to summon up enough energy to speak.

"You were in an accident at the place where you work. You slipped into the pool and needed to be pulled out. You swallowed a lot of water and had to have CPR performed on you at the scene.. By the time the ambulance arrived, you were breathing on your own again." I look over to Rocco and notice that his eyes are beginning to gloss over, as though he's holding back the tears.

"You?" I croak. He gives me a small smile and nods his head a couple of times.

"The only reason you're sitting here with us now is due to the quick actions of this young man right here. If you'd have been in the water any longer or they hadn't started the CPR when they did, I'm not so sure that the paramedics would have been able to revive you in time. He did a really great job today." Rocco's

109

cheeks begin to heat as the doctor glances towards him with a look of awe.

"Thank you." I notice the more I speak, the stronger my voice is becoming. "I don't know how I can ever thank you enough."

"It was nothing, really. You needed help, and I'm really glad that I was the one to be there to help you. I'm glad that you're going to be okay, Mackenzie." He takes hold of my hand and squeezes it gently. There is so much to take in, especially considering I still can't remember anything that happened to me, and if I'm to be completely truthful, this scares me a bit.

"Why can't I remember anything?" I ask Dr Noelle as he writes something down on my notes

"It's perfectly normal when your body goes through something like this. Once your mind thinks you've recovered enough to be able to cope with the memories, it will let them through." I suppose that makes sense, and to be honest I'm not entirely sure if I want to remember if it was as bad as they're making it out to be.

Dr. Noelle continued his checks on me for several more minutes and seemed happy when he left of how I've been progressing.

I feel completely drained. It feels as though I haven't slept in days. I don't even know what the time is. It could be the middle of the night for all I know and going by the darkness outside, it's definitely late. I glance around the room and try to find a clock.

"What are you looking for?" Rocco asks. He's still sitting next to my bed and holding my hand. He hasn't made any attempt to move from where he is.

"I don't know what the time is. I was looking for a clock." I continue to look around the room.

"It's just after two o'clock. Are you tired?"

"Two o'clock? As in two o'clock, in the morning?" I know it's a stupid question considering it's highly unlikely that it would be this dark out in the afternoon.

"Yeah, two in the morning. You've been asleep for about sixteen hours, Makenzie." I look at him to make sure he isn't joking with me. How could I have been out for so long? I try to think back, but the last thing I can remember is the start of my shift at five o'clock. I couldn't have been at work too long before the argument took place. Oh, wait. I remember an argument.

"You were fighting with Josh ..." He lowers his eyes away from mine. I keep my gaze on him because I want to see his face, but he's beginning to look embarrassed and won't look at me.

"Yeah, we were arguing. Can you remember how you ended up in the pool? It was me, Makenzie. I pushed you." His mouth twists unhappily, and he continues to hold his gaze firmly on the floor.

"You pushed me? You pushed me in the pool? Why would you do that?" I can barely get my words out past my tightening throat and can feel the tears brewing in my eyes. I can't believe that he would do that. I know he doesn't know about my fear of the water or anything, but still, to push me in?

"I didn't mean to. You were standing behind me when Josh pushed me and ... I knocked you. I didn't know you were so close behind me. Mackenzie, I'm really, *really* sorry." As he speaks, he brings his eyes back to mine and I can see the pain. I can see that he feels bad about what happened.

"Oh. So you didn't just push me in then?" I say with a small smile reaching my lips. I need to make him feel better. It sounds as though it was an accident, and I'm sure as hell that Rocco wouldn't do anything to intentionally hurt me.

111

"No … well, yeah. But, I honestly didn't know you were there. When you fell in the pool, I stood and waited for you to start swimming back up, but you didn't. You just kept sinking until you hit the bottom of the pool. When I realised that you weren't coming back up to the surface, I think I actually felt my heart stop. I just stood there, and I didn't move. *I couldn't move.* Thankfully, Ben jumped in and pulled you out of the water. When I saw that you weren't breathing, I nearly lost it again but I needed to bring you back. I couldn't lose you." His words shock me. To find out what put me in hospital and what happened to me is bad enough, but to hear what Rocco has been through hurts too. I know all the emotions I felt when I was watching my sister. I tighten my grip on his hand.

"I'm sorry." I whisper to him. He laughs a little at my words.

"Why are you sorry? None of this was your fault, Mackenzie. *None.* I do have one question for you, though. How does someone your age not know how to swim? I swear I feel like I lost about five years off my life today, watching you sink to the bottom of the pool, Makenzie." I lower my head so he doesn't see the embarrassment that I can feel moving into my cheeks again. He doesn't know it, but he's just asked me the only question in the world that I'm not comfortable in answering.

"I don't like the water, so I don't tend to go near it. It seems silly to learn if I don't need too." I hate lying to him, but I can't get the real reason to pass through my lips. Will he think that I'm weak if I was to tell him the real reason for my fear?

"That's it. Once you're feeling better then you and I have a date with a pool. I'll have you swimming in no time." I feel the panic beginning to well up inside me just thinking about being in the water. My breaths become faster than they should be, and I know that Rocco must see the look of fear over my face now.

"I ... no ... I ... can't ... no ..." I stutter as I start to hyperventilate. Rocco stands up quickly from his seat and comes to sit on the bed with me, wrapping his arms around me and holding me close to his chest. I breathe in deeply, inhaling the smell of him as I allow him to soothe me. I really do love the way he smells.

"Hey. Shhhhh. Makenzie, what's wrong? What did I say? I need you to tell me, so I don't say it again." I pull away from his body so I can see into his eyes. He keeps his hands on my hips, and I have to admit, I like it. *A lot*. They're holding me steady, giving me the strength I need for what I'm about to say. I hate talking about this with anyone, including my parents, but he seems to be giving me enough strength just from his touch. Taking a deep breath, I brace myself for the words I'm about to speak.

"My little sister Cassie died in a pool accident ... She was seven ... I watched it happen, but I couldn't do anything about it ... I haven't been in a pool since the day it happened." I feel the tears forming in my eyes, and Rocco pulls me against him again, firmer this time.

"Oh, Makenzie. I'm so sorry. I had no idea. I promise that I won't mention the pool ever again." I smile against his chest, wondering how that will possibly work out for him. Only I, with my extreme fear of pools, could want to date a guy who's a member of a swimming club. This thought makes me giggle softly, making Rocco pull back and eye me strangely.

"Oh, come on! Don't tell me you don't think that this situation isn't just a little bit funny! I have a fear of pools, and you're a member of the swimming team?" He smiles at me, and I can tell that I've managed to lighten the mood. It feels good. The last thing I want is to make Rocco feel awkward, especially after everything he's done for me. I mean, he literally saved my life.

113

"Okay, yeah. I admit the situation is a little unusual."

"My turn to ask a question. What were you and Josh fighting over? I can't remember that part." His laughter abruptly stops, and his cheeks begin to redden again.

"Are you blushing, Rocco?" I laugh a little harder this time as his cheeks become even redder. I don't think I've ever seen Rocco look so embarrassed before now.

"Erm … well … the thing … the thing is … I kinda asked him not to ask you out again. I told him that I was interested, and I wanted to see where this would go …" I feel a sudden burst of warmth making its way through my body from his words. He wants more with me?

"As you can probably gather, he wasn't overly happy about it. I think he likes you, but you know, I really don't care anymore. I told him when you first moved here that I liked you, but it didn't stop him asking you out. None of the guys are used to me actually going after a girl, so I don't really blame him for going ahead and asking you on a date anyway."

"I'm sure you don't have to chase girls, Rocco. I mean, have you looked in the mirror recently?" I can't help the little giggle that follows those words. I mean, who is he trying to kid?

"That's not what I mean. I mean, I don't date." He doesn't date? This sexy guy before me who can have any girl he wants doesn't date?

"What? *Like ever?* But, I saw you. You were out with a girl. The one who was keeping your arm warm with her chest at the restaurant." I try to keep the jealousy out of my voice, but I fail.

Laughing, Rocco answers,

"Oh, yeah. I totally forgot about her. I only went out with her as a favour to Mason. He wanted to take her friend out, but she wouldn't go out without her friend. And, yes I know, she wouldn't stop touching me," Rocco fakes a shudder through his body, which ultimately lessens my jealousy slightly.

"I can't even remember her name, Kim, no Katy? I know this must sounds bad, but the only thing I could focus on that night was you. When you left with Josh after we kissed, I wanted to chase after you and beat the hell out of Josh but Mason wouldn't let me." I watch as the smile crossing his lips get bigger as he tells the story. I remember that moment very clearly. He looked so angry when I left, but I thought that it was because he was angry with me, not Josh.

"When was the last time you went out on a proper date?" I'm enjoying this time with Rocco. It's quiet, just the two of us, and he seems willing to open up to me and I'm more than happy to keep him talking.

"My last date? I think it was when I was with Elle. I haven't been out with anyone since she left. Well, apart from the night we went out dancing." I can't believe that's the only time he's been out since he split up with Elle.

"When did you and she split up?" I still can't believe what he's telling me.

"I would say maybe about a year ago, maybe slightly longer. I can't honestly remember."

"But why haven't you dated? I don't understand." I can see he's starting to get uncomfortable with the questions I'm asking him, but I just can't seem to be able to stop myself. I need to understand why he hasn't been out with anyone.

"I just went through a lot with Elle. I didn't want to be with someone when I was still broken," There he goes with the broken comments again. I really don't know what he means when he talks like this. There's nothing wrong with him, so why would he think this? I'm just about to ask him something else, but the door to my room slams open again. I turn and still my

115

movements. He's the last person in the world that I thought I'd see rushing into my room and looking panicked.

"Makenzie? Oh my god! Are you okay? I was so scared when the hospital called."

Oh God.

"Carl?"

Chapter Twelve

"Carl? What the hell are you doing here?" My voice reveals the shock I'm suffering from seeing Carl rushing into my room. How does he even know that I'm here? More importantly, why is he here? He briskly walks over and stands on the opposite side of the bed that Rocco is sitting on, before wrapping his arms around me and hugging me tightly. Well, this is awkward. *No. This is really awkward.* Rocco still has his hands resting on my hips from when he was just hugging me before Carl entered the room, and now Carl is trying to pull me into his arms too.

"The hospital called. I'm still down on their records as your emergency contact. I was so worried about you, Mackenzie. When they told me that you hadn't woken up yet ..." I mentally curse myself for not changing my details after we parted ways. How could I be so stupid? I've no idea what to do. I mean, this hasn't exactly been the best day I've ever experienced.

I feel Rocco slipping his hands away from my hips and returning to sit back in the chair next to my bed, though it isn't his hands I want removed from my body. I want Carl to take his hands off of me and then just leave.

"I'm fine, Carl. You can go back to Rose now. You really didn't need to come here." I watch as Carls's eyes flicker away from me, and as they land on Rocco, I can see the questioning look within them. In the next moment, he reaches his hand out towards Rocco.

"Sorry, we haven't been introduced. I'm Carl. Mackenzie's fiancé." Rocco's eyes flash towards mine in an instant, and I can already see the realisation flickering into them as he finally puts two and two together.

"EX! You're my *ex* fiancé, Carl. With a very pregnant girlfriend waiting for you at home! You know the one who you got pregnant while we were engaged?" I angrily say while throwing Carl an evil glare.

How dare he still call himself my fiancé? Rocco looks down at Carls hand for a couple of seconds before bringing his gaze back up to his face, refusing to shake his hand. I feel relieved and smile to myself, knowing that there's no way in hell that Rocco will believe anything that Carl has to say.

"I'm gonna leave you guys to it, Makenzie. Give you some time here with your … visitor." I have to try and hold back a laugh when I see Rocco totally blanking Carl, but then what he's just said seems to finally sink in.

"Wait. You don't need to go anywhere. I'm sure Carl is just leaving now that he can see that I'm okay. Aren't you Carl?" I say firmly, while narrowing my eyes over on him.

"Actually, I was planning on staying for a while. I think you and I have some things we need to talk about."

No, no, no. Stop talking!

"No, we don't have anything left to talk about. Rocco, please stay? Carl really is just about to leave." I turn around to Rocco and stare at him with pleading eyes. I don't want to be left alone with Carl. Surely he must see that?

The happiness that was present in his eyes just a few minutes ago has now vanished, and all I can see are the walls I'd finally managed to break down not so long ago, building right back high up around him again.

He's looking at me with distance displaying in his eyes, and I actually feel like I'm about to cry. I know that he's about to shut me out again. I didn't think that it would be possible, but I think I might actually hate Carl more in this very moment than I did during the entire time we were dealing with the Rose scenario.

"No, I really think that it would be for the best if I leave. I hope you feel better soon, Mackenzie" With these words, he turns and begins to walk away, and I can only watch as he leaves the room, taking a part of my heart with him. I glare towards Carl. He's lucky that I'm attached to all of these drips and machines because if I wasn't, I'd be out of this hospital bed, and the staff would have to pry my hands from around his throat.

"Have you lost your freaking mind?"

"Who was he, Makenzie?" I can't believe that he has the audacity to look upset about me having Rocco in the room.

"It doesn't matter who he is. Why the hell are you here?" I'm getting angrier by the minute, and not just at Carl. I'm mad with Rocco for running away again. What do I have to say to him so he'll believe that I want him. That I want *all of him*, damaged pieces and all?

"I would like to know who the guy in my fiancées room is. I don't think it's too much to ask, is it?" I tilt my head to the side and look directly at him so I can study him. He doesn't look as though he's on drugs, but he must be. It's the only way to explain any of this.

"I swear, Carl! If you call me your fiancée one more time then I'm going to get out of this bed and beat you with my own bare fists!" He looks surprised, though I have no idea why. He looks as though he's about to say something, but I'm saved by the sound of the door as it begins to open. I'm hoping that Rocco has changed his mind, but he hasn't. Walking in is the nurse, Elizabeth.

"The doctor will be here soon to do another check of everything and he said that if everything is still okay, then you'll be free to go. Do you have a way to get home?" She asks as she smiles at me. If she'd have been twenty five minutes earlier then I could have said yes, but now it seems that I'm stranded here.

"Yes, I'll give her a lift home. Do I need to sign any paperwork?" The nurse looks over at Carl, most probably wondering who he is. So far, the only visitor I've had has been Rocco.

"I'm perfectly capable of signing my own damn forms! I'm a grown woman!" I snap at him and then I close my eyes, letting out a deep sigh as I try to calm myself back down.

"But ... thank you for offering to give me a lift." I look at him again, and though he's smiling, it doesn't make me feel happy in the slightest. He looks as though he has just gotten his way, and that I will fall into his arms because he came to the hospital. He has a rude awakening coming.

"A lift, Carl. That's all." He nods his head and gives me a tiny salute. Funny how I always used to think that it was really cute when he did that. Now, well it just annoys the hell out of me.

Sitting in the car with Carl on the way home feels strange. I've spent the last few months trying to get over him and move on with my life, and here I am, in his company again. I sit quietly and look out the side window because I have no idea what to say to him, and honestly, all I can think about is getting rid of him so I can speak with Rocco.

Discharging myself from the hospital had taken a long time, and now I'm tired. My body still hurts, and now my head is beginning to hurt from having to deal with Carl. I just want to get home, call Rocco, and then curl up in my own bed so I can sleep for about four days.

Matt had called while I was still in the hospital, and he told me that if I returned to work this week then he would fire me. I suppose this means I'll be resting a lot over the next week. I have a smile over my face while I think about Matt. He really does feel like a father figure to me. He's sweet and always looking out for me. He sounded so upset because I hadn't told him about my water phobia. I think he thinks that if he'd known, then maybe it wouldn't have happened.

I assured him that it was entirely my fault. There was no way for him to have been able to change what had happened. He informed me that he's planning on having words with Rocco and Josh, so maybe it's a good thing that I won't be in this week, after all. I know Rocco feels really bad about what happened, and he completely blames himself. When Matt has words, I think that it's he's going to make him feel even worse.

"Where can I park, Makenzie?" My thoughts are interrupted by the sound of Carl's voice. I forgot he was here, or maybe that's just wishful thinking on my part.

"You can just stop outside my door and drop me at the kerb. You don't need to park." He looks at me with confusion on his face, as though I've just spoken to him in a foreign language.

"I'm not dropping you off in the street. I wasn't kidding when I said I wanted to talk to you, and since you've managed to avoid any sort of conversation with me so far, it will have to be at your place." I manage to hold in the groan that I feel ready to escape from my throat. I really don't want this to happen. Why can't he just drop me off and disappear into the sunset, and back to Rose? I actually feel my lip curling up into a snarl when I think of her.

"Carl, I'm tired and I just want to go to bed. We have nothing to talk about. Nothings changed." Even as I speak, he parks the car next to the kerb just across the street from my apartment. I groan as I climb out of the car, praying that he'll change his mind and drive away. I completely ignore him as I cross the street and make my way up the stairs. I'm hoping that he'll take the hint and leave, but he doesn't. I unlock my door, step inside, but just as I'm about to close it, he puts his hand against the door, stopping me being able to close it fully.

"You're not stopping this from happening, Makenzie. You can either let me come in now and speak to you, or I can wait out here on your doorstep until you're ready to hear me out." I let my head drop, thinking that maybe I should just let him have his say so he'll leave.

"Fine. You have thirty minutes, Carl. I move away from the door, not even holding it open for him so he can step inside. I make my way over to the sofa while removing my jacket. I sit down wearily and curl my legs under me. Pulling the blanket I keep over the back of the sofa over my legs, I make myself a little more comfortable. I look to Carl, who's now sitting down on the chair opposite to me. He's taken off his jacket, which makes me worry that he's planning on staying longer than I want him to. He stares at me for a few minutes, and he's beginning to make me feel uncomfortable. I'm about to say something to him, but stop when he finally gets to the point.

"I fucked up, Makenzie." If Carl is going for the shock factor with this conversation then he's doing a pretty good job at it. I know he screwed up badly, but I'd never imagined that he would openly admit it.

"I can't believe that I did that to you. You were my everything, Mackenzie" I open my mouth to stop him from saying anything else, but he holds his hand up, silencing me.

"I had everything, but at the time I thought that I needed more, that I needed the thrill of the chase again. But, now I realise that what I needed was you all along. Rose ... she just *isn't you*. I'm so sorry I put you through this, but I want you back. Please say you'll have me? I'm ready to pack up my life and leave Rose. Say it. Just say that you'll come home with me." I stare at him with my mouth hanging wide open, I have no idea what to say. But, then it happens. I feel it building inside me and no matter how hard I try, I can't stop it. I laugh. I mean, I seriously laugh. What else am I supposed to do? He cheated on me, got the woman pregnant, and now he's willing to leave her and come back to me? My life right now feels as though it's just turned into some Hollywood movie.

"You seriously think I'm going to come back to you, Carl? That I'm going to allow you to leave your PREGNANT girlfriend so that I can have her sloppy seconds? I don't think so. If you'd loved me so much in the first place then you never would have cheated on me. What's wrong? Is the grass not greener on the other side like you'd thought it would be?" I should feel angry, but I don't. I actually feel sorry for him. He lost everything that we had together and has finally realised that he made a big mistake

"Makenzie, please? It has always been you. *Always*. I don't know if I can do this without you."

"Maybe you should have thought about that before you started dipping it in company ink! You made your choice, Carl, and it wasn't me. The first time that you went with her was the first time you told me you didn't want me anymore. I'm not coming back. I'm really happy with my life now. I'm happy here, and I'm happy with my friends." I need to get it through to him that I'm not leaving here, especially not to be with him. I am happy. Happier than I think I've ever been in my life.

"It's because of him, isn't it? He's the reason you won't come home." I close my eyes and begin to rub my fingers lightly over my temples. I can already sense that this headache won't be leaving me anytime soon.

"No, Carl. Let me explain this to you so you can easily understand. I'm not coming back to you because you cheated on me. You have a pregnant girlfriend at home. I will never be with you again, and it has nothing to do with Rocco. This is my life now, and I'm happy." I say this all very slowly and clearly, hoping that he'll finally hear and understand what I'm telling him. I don't want to be horrible to him, no matter what he put me through. I know only too well how it feels to lose something you want so badly.

"You need to go home, Carl. Go back and enjoy the life you chose for yourself. It can't be as bad as you're making it sound. You have a baby on the way, and you said it yourself, you always wanted to have children." His head drops down, and he stares at his hands which are now grasped together in front of him on his lap.

"Yeah. But, now I realise that I wanted to have that family with you. It's just not the same with Rose. She doesn't know me the way you do. I wasn't meant to be with her. I'm meant to be with you. *Always, you..*" I can hear the pain in his voice, but it doesn't change anything. This is all still fully on him.

"Do you know that she fell pregnant on purpose?" My jaw drops when he utters this statement. I knew there was a reason I hated her, but now I really hate her. How could anyone do that to another person?

"Oh my God, Carl. You can't be serious? How do you know this?"

"She told me." He chuckles right after he drops this bomb. But, it isn't a happy sound. He sounds broken, and I can feel my heart going out to him.

"She asked me to leave you … not long after we first started sleeping together. I told her that it would never happen. I told her there was no way that I would leave you, so she stopped taking her pill. I was stupid to believe she had everything covered. Once she was pregnant, there was nothing else I could do. I wouldn't leave her on her own, not when she was carrying my kid, but God Makenzie, it's hard. She isn't the person I thought she was, she's … well, she's a bitch!"

"Carl, I'm so sorry. I really am, but even if I was willing to come back to you it still wouldn't change anything. She would still be there between us. You need to deal with the life you chose, and you need to do it without me. I'm not ever going to come back to you." His shoulders drop low, and I know that he has finally started to hear me.

"I know. But, damn I had to try. Surely you can't blame me for that, can you? This time the smile that appears on his face seems genuine, not forced like before.

"Just know that I'll always love you, Makenzie. If you ever need me, I'll always be here for you." I feel tears appearing in my eyes as he speaks. This is the Carl I used to know and love. The one who cares with his whole heart and doesn't want anyone to ever be hurting.

"I know, but it just wasn't meant to be. You'll always be my first love, Carl. You're just not going to be my last love, that's all." He looks up at me, and it's as though he's seeing me for the first time.

"Yeah, I see that. So, do you love him?" I look directly into his eyes and say with the conviction that I haven't felt in a long time.

"No, not yet. But, I think he may be the last person that I will love." It's more than I've even admitted to myself, and it feels liberating to finally admit my feelings to someone. To let it out into the universe that I'm falling for Rocco in a big way. That I'm truly not going to give up on him or let him run away from me again. Rocco Cole had better watch out because I'm not willing to let him go.

Carl stands up from the chair and grabs his jacket. Walking over to me, he crouches down before placing a feather light kiss on my right cheek.

"Be happy, Makenzie. I hope he gives you everything that I couldn't. But I'm always at the end of the phone if need me." With those words, he walks away, leaving me on the sofa.

I hear the front door close behind him and know that it might be the last time I ever see Carl. I know I should feel sad, but I don't. He's a part of the life I'm trying to leave behind me. Now is the time to fully start living the life I want, starting with me kicking the arse of an extremely infuriating man.

I pick up my phone and dial Mason's number. I know Rocco won't pick up, so there isn't any point in attempting to call him. Sorting things with him will need to be done face to face, so he has no way of avoiding me. He needs to know exactly what I'm thinking and how infuriating I find him.

"Hello?"

"Mason? It's Makenzie." I'm not sure how much to tell him, but I know that I need to get Rocco's address from him. *That is a must.*

"Makenzie, how are you doing? I heard about what happened. Shit, I can't believe you nearly died!" That's what I like the most about Mason. He doesn't have a filter. He just tells you how it is and exactly what's on his mind. Most people would try and be gentle about what happened, but no, not Mason. He's just straight in there with the bad stuff.

"I'm fine. A little tired just now, but I feel okay. I'm actually calling you for a favour.

"Anything you need, Makenzie. You know that." I smile. Mason may be a big man whore, but he really does have a heart of gold deep down.

"I need Rocco's address."

126

"But isn't Rocco with you? I thought he was at the hospital?" I can feel my anger beginning to build again, but try my hardest to push it back down. It's not Mason's fault that Rocco is immensely frustrating.

"No, Mason. Rocco left the hospital a little while ago, and I need his address so I can go and kick his arse." The sound of booming laughter travels through the line. Well, at least someone's finding this whole situation amusing.

"Damn, woman. I knew there was a reason why I like you so much. You're just what Rocco needs. Someone to knock him into shape and stop him from hiding from the world."

"I hope you're right on this one, Mason. What I do know is that I'm not giving up on him without a fight. So, are you going give me his address or not?" Mason laughs again before giving me Rocco's address.

"Thanks, Mason. I owe you one."

"Makenzie, if you can get Rocco back to living properly, then I'll I owe you ten!" With that comment, we say our goodbyes.

I lean myself against the back of the sofa with exhaustion. There has been so much drama over the past few days, and even though I slept for the best part of the last twenty four hours, it all seems to be catching up with me now.

There's no way that I'm going to be able to go over to Rocco's house and have it out with him while I'm feeling like this. I know I need to sleep before I head out.

I lay down and curl up on the sofa, pulling the blanket up to my chin. I close my eyes and begin to think about everything that's happened, still trying to get my head around it all. The rate of my breathing increases slightly as I think about the accident. *I almost died.* Actually, if what the doctor said is true, then I had died. It wasn't until Rocco resuscitated me that I began breathing again. He saved my life. And I don't mean in the love story he

127

saved my life way, I mean in the 'he really made me breath again' saved my life way.

He's my real life hero. My knight in shining armour. Thinking about Rocco has calmed my breathing and my body is beginning to relax as my nerves settle.

I've never had someone in my life who has had such an effect on me before, not just the chemistry between us messing with my hormones, but he can actually calm me. Make me feel safer than ever before. The last thought going through my mind before I finally drift off is one of Rocco, with his dark hair and eyes, the thought of the smile he gives me when he's turned on, the one that makes my toes curl. The one who I'm making it my mission to see more of, whether Rocco knows it yet or not.

Chapter Thirteen

My day had started so dreadfully, and it just seemed to go downhill as the day progressed. It started bad when I woke up this morning after 9am, normally I would be happy to have a long lie but this was the last thing I had expected. My few hours' nap the day before had turned into close to 12 hours of sleep…on my sofa. So not only had I missed my chance to go to Rocco's last night, I also woke up with a sore neck. Not only was I annoyed that I never made it to his house, but I had been determined to set things right before any unpleasant pictures of Carl and me had the chance to run too wild in his mind.

After showering and getting dressed I sat wondering what to do. I wanted to talk to Rocco, but I knew he would be at work, I already knew he had a week of meetings at work, so a quick search later and I left my apartment with the address of the garage in my phone. It was quite a ways away on foot, but it didn't bother me, I had dressed casually in a short denim skirt, blue halter-top and a pair of low tops, so a walk with the wind against my face and the fresh air was a welcome treat. I was about half way into my twenty-minute walk when the heavens opened, we hadn't had rain for weeks, so I hadn't even thought to bring a jacket. And that's how I got where I am now, standing in the forecourt of Rocco's garage looking like a drowned rat.

I wasn't sure what to do now, no matter how much I want to talk to him, did I really want to see him when I looked like such a mess? But the thought of walking home again in the rain, (and knowing my luck today) catching pneumonia, just wasn't an appealing thought. I'm stuck in my head trying to make a decision, but the sudden sound of laughter sliced through my thoughts. I look up to see Mason standing in the open garage door, doubled over with his hands on his knees, laughing so hard that tears run down his cheeks. The indecision is back, but for a totally different reason. Now I need to decide where I'm going to punch Mason, my vote at the moment is that really sensitive area between his legs. I clench my fists and storm over to where he is standing, the look on my face must be one of murder as he raises his hands and backs away from me quickly.

"Don't, Makenzie. I didn't mean to laugh. Dammit woman don't hit me." He may be saying all the right words, but the laughing hasn't stopped yet.

"Really, Mason? I shouldn't hit you when you are finding the fact that I'm drenched absolutely hilarious. I have had a shit day, and I need to relieve some tension. Hitting you would be the best cure at the moment." I can hear the anger in my voice, even though I wasn't trying to sound quite as stabby. Definitely a bad day!

"Nope. Not gonna be your punching bag. I only let women do that in bed, but you know…if you're offering?" He wiggles his eyebrows suggestively, but that does nothing to help. Not even his smile and wink will get me out of this mood. A door creaks open, and I turn as I hear his voice.

"Mason. What the he…" He notices me standing there and stops mid-sentence. God knows how disastrous I look at this moment, I know rain still dripping down my face. Rocco starts to back up slightly like he will be able to just disappear into the shadows.

"Don't even try it!" I point a finger at him, so he knows exactly who I'm talking to. He stops in his tracks and looks towards Mason with a look that is asking for help.

"I'm sorry dude, but you're on your own with this one." With this Mason walks back to the work area returning to the bikes being worked on. This is the first of me noticing that there happened to be an audience of dudes watching us, looking at me with a mixture of amusement and something that looks like worry. I feel the blush working up my cheeks, who knows what they must be thinking about this mad woman standing soaking wet and shouting at both their bosses.

I point at Rocco again, "We need to talk. Now."

"Oh...em...ok. Is my office ok?" I nod my head, and he stands back to let me walk past him. His office is not what I expected. Working in the garage I expected to see lots of grease, bike parts and for it to look a bit run down but that's not what I get. To start with, it's actually quite large. There is an enormous dark wood desk taking up a good portion of the room, I'm not sure any one person needs a desk of that magnitude. He must hold a lot of meetings in here with the professional look that the room has, but then I have never seen Rocco looking anything less than perfect so I shouldn't expect his office to look any different. Hearing the door close behind me I turn and look at him, and as much as I try not to look over him I just can't stop myself. He looks good in anything he wears but in a suit with the sleeves rolled up, showing just a little of his tattoo, he is almost edible. I give my head a shake to clear my mind, I'm not here to look at him, I'm here to kick his arse.

"You walked out on me again, Rocco." I'm happy that I manage to get the words out strong. He looks at me for a moment longer before walking away, leaving the office through a different door. I stand there with my mouth open, not believing that he is actually walking away from me *again*. Before I have a chance to shout after him, he re-appears through the door holding a towel in his hand. He hands it to me as he walks over to his desk and grabs something out of a drawer. I am drying my hair when he comes back to stand in front of me, it doesn't escape my notice that he still hasn't spoken to me.

"Here. You look cold." He holds out a white t-shirt with the garages name 'RM's Custom Fits', on the front.

"I'm fine, Rocco. I will dry off soon."

"Makenzie, you can't keep that top on. You will end up ill, especially after what you have just been through." His voice takes on a slight edge to it.

"Rocco, I..." I'm not able to finish what I am saying before he has me turned towards the door, pushing me through it by the shoulders.

"I'm not gonna speak to you until you get your top changed, Makenzie. So stop fighting me, and just do it." With those parting words, he closes the door, leaving me alone in a small bathroom. I stand there mutely with a t-shirt in my hands, glaring at the door he has just closed. Well, damn him. He will just have to deal with it. He won't talk to me until I'm wearing it then I will wear it, and hope I don't die of embarrassment while I prove a point.

With the fresh shirt in place, I stomp from the bathroom; I refuse to admit to Rocco that I'm grateful to be feeling warmer. Rocco is sitting, waiting, on the edge of his desk with a cup of coffee in his hand. His long legs are stretched out in front of him, I wonder how it's possible that he seems so comfortable with himself, I am always a little awkward no matter who I am around. I'd kill for just a shred of that inner comfort. My arms crossed over the front of my body, I can already feel the blush on my cheeks.

"Here. This will help warm you up." Little does he know, that when he is around me my body is always warm.

"Thank you. If you put it on the table, I will get it in a minute."

"Damn it, Makenzie. Stop being so bloody defiant." I stand there in shock. He thinks I'm being defiant? Who the hell does he think he is? Fine I will take his bloody cup of coffee. I drop my arms and reach out to take the cup. I register the instant he notices the reason for my "bloody defiance," as he so kindly calls it. His eyes drop down to my chest and rapidly darken to a smouldering gaze I can't look away from. I can feel his stare on my breasts, and it's making my nipples tighten under the thin layer of the T-shirt. He has just learnt the unspoken rule among women, that you can't wear a bra under a halter-top. At the same time, I learn that I have absolutely no control over my body when he is about. He hasn't stopped staring since I moved my hands.

"Rocco, my face is up here." His head whips up as he looks at my face instead of my chest. I see a reddening blush creep into his face, but it doesn't remove the lust I can see in his eyes. If he wants me as much as his body claims to, why does he keep running away?

"Damn. Yeah, sorry. You...em...wanted to talk?" He manages to stutter out while focusing intently on my face. I take a step towards him, and he pulls his legs back in so I don't trip.

"I want to know the truth, why did you walk out again?" His shoulders dropped a little, and I hear him sigh. He turns slightly and places the cup on his desk, turning back to me he explains.

"I couldn't be there with him. I want to hurt him for what he put you through, for the pain he caused you. And watching him touch you was just driving me insane. He still wants you, Makenzie." I move closer to him again, forcing him to spread his knees apart.

"I know he does, but I don't want him. There was only one person in that room that I wanted to touch me, and he left me there...*again*." He is watching my lips as I talk, his tongue licking

133

over his own. This talk isn't going the way I wanted it to. I came here to kick his ass and all I can think about is kissing him.

"He's your fiancé." He whispers, his lips so close to mine.

"Ex." I brush my nose over Rocco's and I hear him inhale deeply. I can feel him trying to resist, trying to not give into what is between us. His hands reach out and grab me by the hips pulling me further into him. I place my hands on his chest, playing with the buttons of his shirt. He always feels so good; so warm and hard under my hands.

"He still wants you though. I don't want to get in between the two of you."

"There is nothing to get between, Rocco. The only person I wanted there yesterday is the stubborn man that is trying *really* hard not to kiss me right now." That's the final push that Rocco needs to finally put his lips on mine. I swallow the groan from him as I open my mouth, allowing him all the access he wants. His hands grip harder as I move fully against him, letting every inch of our bodies press together. Grinding gently into the now prominent erection in his trousers, I feel more confident about the plan to make him mine. His kiss dominates me, there is more need and passion in this one kiss than any of the others that we have shared. His lips mark me, making me his even if he doesn't even realise it. I pull back from the kiss slightly, taking his bottom lip between my teeth and pulling gently. His eyes close as he lets a little growl out, placing his head against mine he mutters,

"Makenzie, you keep doing things like that and I won't be able to stop myself from what I do next."

"Who says I want you to stop?" I challenge him. Daring him to take me the way we both crave. He looks at me for another moment before grabbing me tightly at the waist, lifting me completely and turning before placing me where he had been sitting on his desk.

"You really do like to challenge me at every opportunity, don't you?" I reach up and loosen the tie from around his neck, pulling it over his head, letting it drop to the floor.

Starting to unbutton his shirt I say to him,

"There is no challenge here, Rocco. I am right here in front of you to do with as you please. I don't know how to tell you any clearer than I have," I lean forward and place kisses on his chest in between my words.

"I," Kiss.

"Want," Kiss.

"You." Kiss.

Rocco's head has dropped back as I work my way down his body letting my lips work their magic. Reaching the bottom button, I pull the shirt out of his trousers. He brings his head up and watches me as I push the shirt from his shoulders, making it land next to his tie on the floor. I take a minute to look over him, standing there in just his trousers. His chest is going up and down as his breathing is getting harsher, and his eyes haven't left mine. He reaches forward and grabs the hair at the back of my head, bringing my lips close to his.

"You are going to make me lose the only control I ever thought I had. I can't think when you touch me." His words, along with the hold he has on my hair is making me wet. I can feel the muscles in my core tighten as he tangles his hands in my hair even more.

"I want you, Makenzie. More than I've ever wanted anyone before. Are you willing to accept everything from me? All of my flaws? All of it, even if I can't give you everything I should?" I try to form words, but he has stolen all the breath from my body. I feel like I'm drowning in all the thoughts and emotions flooding through me. He pulls my head back more, taking the skin of my neck just the way I yearned.

"I asked you a question, Makenzie. Can you accept me with everything I can, and everything I can't give you? Do you want me?" I hear a squeak leave my throat as I feel my body hurtling towards orgasm. He hasn't even touched me and I feel like I'm losing the fight against my release. Every time he says my name, it feels like he is running his tongue between my legs. My breath shudders as he moves in and runs his nose up my neck smelling me. When did I lose the power in this seduction?

"I want anything I can get from you, Rocco. I want everything you can give me and the things you can't I won't even miss." He releases his hold on my hair and I can finally look him in the eyes. He has a strange look deep within them, almost like fear but I have no idea why he would be afraid.

"Do you know what you're asking for? I haven't been with anyone since my accident, not even Elle. I don't know if I can anymore."

And there it is. The truth of everything that is going through his head. The fears that have been making him run from me. I feel a lump in my throat when I realise how much it took him to say those words to me, to admit his biggest fear aloud. I will not let this moment pass without showing him how un-broken he is. Leaning forward I let me breath wash over his lips as I reach down and cup his still present erection in my hand.

"It sure doesn't feel like there is a problem with anything working. I think it feels amazing and I haven't even felt it in the flesh yet." Rocco's head bumps against mine and his eyes close.

"Fuck, Makenzie." He gasps against my lips. I let my hands move to his belt buckle slowly, giving him a chance to stop me if he needs to. I don't want to push him too hard, not now that he is finally letting his walls come down. I pop the top button on a moan, I don't think I have ever been so turned on in my life. I have wanted men in the past but I *need* Rocco. His lips press

136

onto mine gently, I know the connection of our lips is important to him, making him feel more grounded. I know this as I feel exactly the same way. I lower his zipper, feeling the pressure of his hardness on my fingers. I don't know how he didn't break the zip. I rub my hand up the outside of his boxer shorts and along the outline of him. A groan comes from Rocco and it's my turn to shudder. Now that I am this close to his hardness, and even though I have been this close before, it's not enough. *I need it all.* I push his trousers down over his hips lightly, giving me better access to what I am desperate for. I pull the front of his boxers away, I can feel him tense where his body is against me. He feels like a bow, strung tight and ready to release the tension at any moment. My heart is racing as I take this…this whatever it is, further than we have before. I wrap my fingers around his erection and gently rub him from root to tip.

"Oh God. Makenzie, oh my god." he chants as his head drops forward and leans on my chest. I continue to trace my hand up and down his length, feeling him shudder and jump in my hand. Without lifting his head I feel his hands grip at the edge of the t-shirt I'm wearing, roughly pulling it up my body, until I have no option but let him go and lift my arms so he can take it off me. He throws it to the floor where we are building a pile of clothing, once it is clear from my head and before I am able to focus again his lips attack mine. His tongue is hot against mine, exploring my mouth and sucking on my tongue. I wrap my fingers in his hair and pull him closer, trying to lose myself in his body; wanting him to lose himself in mine just as much. I feel his hands move up my sides, rubbing little patterns on my skin, as he gets closer to where I want to feel his hands. I hold my breath as his smooth gentle hands finally make contact with my breasts, gently massaging them, his thumb rubbing over my already hard nipples.

"Rocco." I manage to pant into his mouth. The sensations swirling through my body are becoming too hard to handle, I feel everything that he is doing to me. His tongue and his hand making a lethal combination for my nerves. Now that I have parted my lips from him, he kisses over my jaw, down my neck, over my shoulder and down my chest towards my breasts. Taking my nipple into his mouth a rough gasp erupts as I have to work hard to keep the orgasm I feel, from happening. His tongue has a direct line to my core and I feel everything intensifying in the bottom of my belly and I know it won't take much to push me past the point of no return. Grabbing Rocco's hair I mean to pull his head away, to give me some relief from his mouth, but what I do instead is push him closer to my body, arching my back, pushing my breasts closer to him. I can't get enough but I know this may be too much very soon.

"Rocco. You need to stop. I can't take anymore." He pulls his mouth away from my breast but tugs my nipple with his teeth.

"Why?" He growls out in a rasp that I have never heard him use before, and immediately returns his mouth to my other breast.

"Oh God. Please, Rocco, stop. My body is about to explode." And I'm not lying to him, my body is right on the edge now, every nerve is so sensitive that I think I am about to spontaneously combust. Rocco doesn't listen to me though, the hand that isn't being used to hold my breast to his mouth runs down my body. He lifts my skirt as he trails his fingers trail up the inside of my thigh. I throw my head back and stare at the ceiling, hoping that if I can't see what he is doing to me I might be able to calm down. I am proven wrong when he slips his fingers into my panties, running the length of me.

"Oh God, Makenzie. You're so fucking wet." I've never heard Rocco talk like this, or take so much control, and it's turning me on so much. He's surprised I'm so wet, and I'm surprised I haven't melted to a puddle on the floor. With a mind of its own my body strains to get closer to him, to feel him bringing me the pleasure it needs. I hear a small laugh from him before he sinks two fingers into my heat making me grip the edge of the desk, I feel like I need to stop myself from floating into the air.

Lifting my head so I can watch what he is doing, and I realise quickly what a bad idea that it truly is. Watching his fingers disappear into me has my muscles clenching around his fingers, and grinding my hips into the palm of his hand that is lined up perfectly to my clit. I look up and find him watching me, his breathing almost as laboured as mine and his eyes dark with need. Just looking at the way he looks now, full of passion and an obvious need to take me, is all it takes to push me over the edge into my release. I throw my head back and moan his name as fireworks go off through my body, every muscle tensing as I shake with the best orgasm of my life. Coming down from the euphoria that I have just experienced I realise that Rocco has been talking to me. I try to get my brain to function so I can work out what he has been saying.

"You are so beautiful when you orgasm. You're gorgeous all the time but when you're flushed like that and look like you have just had the time of your life...well that is just something else." He places small kisses against my lips.

"So beautiful." He sounds in awe of what has just happened, and he isn't the only one. I know one thing for certain, in this moment, I need this man more than I need my next breath. I lean forward so my lips are next to his ear and I whisper, in what I hope is a seductive voice,

"I want you, Rocco. No, I need you. Now. I want you to bend me over this desk and take from me what you want. I have had mine, now it's your turn." I wondered when I got the confidence to talk like this. I have never been the type of person to take the lead when it comes to sex, I was just always the partner willing to go along with what the other wanted. He just stares at me, likes he's trying to work out what to do. I reach down and rub along the erection that is still very prominent in his boxers. His eyes roll, and he lets out such a sexy groan, and even though I have just had an incredibly intense release I can feel the muscles in my stomach start to tighten again.

"Fuck me, Rocco." All remnants of control seem to flee from Rocco, and he grabs my waist and pulls me from the desk. He turns me around and pushes until my legs hit the edge of the desk. Standing there, my back against his chest, feeling the warmth flowing from his naked body, he whispers.

"I think I'm about to prove that everything with my body still works." I swear that if he weren't holding me up I would collapse to the floor. Those are the sexiest words he could have said to me, telling me he is about to give me everything that I crave. He places a hand between my shoulder blades and pushes me down, until I feel my nipples brush against the desk. I'm lying with my chest lying flat on the desk, feeling more turned on than I thought possible, just knowing what is about to happen.

"Oh, look. I'm not the only person with tattoos. Damn, Makenzie, do you know how sexy that is?" I feel his fingers trace down my back, following the swirls of my tattoo as they run down my spine. Reaching my skirt he lifts it up over my hips, leaving only my panties and his boxers between us. I feel his lips on my back, kissing back up my body. When he reaches my shoulders, his body flush with mine, he bites me gently while grabbing onto the side of my panties.

"Are you ready for this, Makenzie? Are you sure you want this?" I need to slow my breathing, I feel like I'm starting to hyperventilate. I focus on taking deep breaths, not on what Rocco is saying.

"Makenzie?" He asks as he still his hands.

"Yes, Rocco. Please." Placing another kiss on my shoulder, he starts to lower my panties…as his office door opens wide and a voice I don't want to hear starts talking.

"So did you two get things…shit! Oh man. Sorry!" Mason stutters and he quickly turns his back to the sight that has met him inside the office.

"Mason! Don't just turn around. Leave!" This just seems to make Mason laugh. I don't know what to do, I'm lying across Rocco's desk half-dressed and Mason still hasn't closed the door.

"I'm serious, Mason. You have ten seconds to leave before I lose my shit." Rocco grabs the t-shirt from the floor and stands in front of me until I manage to cover at least my chest with it. He gives me a gentle kiss on the nose,

"Go get dressed in the bathroom, I will get rid of this idiot before you come out." I decide that an escape sounds like a fantastic idea, so I just about run into the bathroom. As I make it to the door, Mason calls to me.

"Makenzie?"

"What?" I snapped unnecessarily; it sounded bitchy, but I really didn't want to be standing here half naked and have a conversation.

"Nice tattoo." I hear his laughter as I turn quickly and slam the door to the bathroom. The last thing I hear is Rocco's angry voice.

"What the fuck, Mason?"

I quickly pull the t-shirt over my head and look at myself in the mirror. What I see is much better than the first time I came in here. After being caught in the rain on the way here, I had been horrified to find what I had looked like. My hair was no longer a lovely wavy style, it looked more like a wet birds nest, straggly and messy. My makeup hadn't faired any better, leaving me looking like a distant relative of a panda, just not that cute. This time there is not the same wet mess, what I see is my flushed cheeks and bright eyes. I smile a little to myself, remembering exactly what had put the blush on my cheeks. Feeling more composed, and a lot more dressed, I open the door and re-enter the office. Looking about seeing who is here, but I can't see anyone, including Rocco. I'm not sure what I'm supposed to do, do I leave? Do I wait? Would Rocco want me to leave after being caught by Mason? Is that why he left, to give me a chance to leave without being embarrassed again? But he kissed me, would he do that if he wanted me to go? I am interrupted from my inner turmoil by the office door opening and Rocco walking in. He doesn't look upset, in fact, he has a huge grin on his face as he approaches me. When he reaches me, he wraps his arms around my waist.

"Well, that was...well it was unexpected but amazing." He says before placing a gentle kiss on my lips.

"What? Mason catching us or what was happening before?" I can't help but laugh, if I don't laugh I might go into hiding for the rest of my life.

"Definitely what was happening before. As for Mason catching us, well I wouldn't expect to live that down for a while. But I think it was totally worth it." He kisses my nose again. This was fast becoming our sweet ritual, and I loved it a little more each time he did it.

"Oh God. He's going to tell everyone isn't he?"

"I wouldn't use the word going to, he has already told all the workers. That's where I went, I needed to threaten him with

142

bodily harm if he didn't stop. Not that I think it has actually made any difference." I drop my head so it's on Rocco's chest.

"Ugh. I can never show my face ever again." Rocco laughs at me, obviously not realising that, at this moment, I am being very serious. I look up at his face, I need to see his reaction to my next question.

"So where does this leave us? I really didn't expect what happened today, not that I regret it, but I did come here to just speak to you. Actually, I came here to kick your arse for walking away from me again...and leaving me to get a lift home with Carl." I give him an angry scowl, but I don't think it's very scary since he laughs again.

"I'm sorry. I just didn't want to get in to the middle of something. I have a lot of damage from my time with Elle that I would bring to a relationship, and I don't think you realise how much."

"How could I know, Rocco? You won't tell me, you won't let me know what you're dealing with. I have as much drama as you, but I want to be with you. You need to let me in, I'm not doing all this chasing and then ending up without you." Damn this man is so hard headed. I need him to start hearing what I'm saying. I don't know how many more times I could possibly tell him I want him. All of him.

"I thought it was the men who are meant to do all the chasing?"

"Then chase me, Rocco. I promise not to run, I'll let you catch me." His arms tighten around my waist, and that beautiful smile appears, the one that only surfaces when he is truly happy.

"You really are everything a guy could ask for, aren't you? I want to move forward with you, today was a mistake," I go to interrupt him, how can he think that today was a mistake, but he places a kiss against my lips.

"It was a mistake as when I'm finally with you, I want it to be after I have told you everything. I want to let you know everything that I am dealing with, why I keep running. Once I have told you, hopefully that will make it easier for you to understand me, and I will be able to get past what is stopping me. After I have told you those things, Makenzie, then nothing will stop me from being with you." Thank God! It is my turn to smile, his words soothing the feeling I had that we would never be together.

"Deal. So how soon can we have this chat, because I really want to be with you, Rocco. How about tonight?"

"I really wish I could, but I need to leave for work for a few days. I have meetings with a supplier in London. Maybe next time you could give me a few days' notice before you try and seduce me in my office." I hit him on the chest and laugh.

"I didn't plan to seduce you. You just look so damn good in your suit, and then once you started with the dirty talk, well I was a goner." He actually blushes. There seems to be two different sides to Rocco, the sweet guy like I have now, and the hot in control guy that I get when he is turned on.

"Yeah, well, you seem to bring that out in me. I have never felt the need to have someone as strongly as I do when I'm with you. And the growling...not sure where that comes from." He laughs. It's nice to know that he has as little control as I do, but with that I feel a little more disappointed that we were interrupted by Mason. Ok, truthfully, I'm a lot more disappointed.

"Don't be embarrassed, I love it. There is nothing better for a girl's ego than a guy losing control. I'm just sad that I didn't get to return the favour and you know...ease some of your tension." I feel a small blush creeping up my cheeks. Now that we aren't in the act I seem to have developed my filter again and I find it difficult to talk about it.

"I got more than you will ever know out of what just happened. Do I wish we had been able to finish? Yes, most definitely, but I'm just going to have to wait to enjoy you fully. And I will enjoy you fully." His lips brush over mine in a deeper kiss this time, it feels like he is letting me know how much he desires me with the way his lips move in sync with mine. I'm growing addicted to Rocco's kisses, now that he seems to give them to me freely, I want his lips on me constantly. Wrapped in his arms with his lips on mine, there is no better place in this world to be.

I leave the garage in a much better mood than I had arrived in. The rain has stopped and I finally feel things with Rocco are moving in the direction they are meant to. We have organised to meet in a few nights time when he returns from his trip. He isn't sure when exactly he will be back but he promises to call me while he is away, and if he doesn't I will be sitting at his front door when he returns home, he will not escape me this time.

Chapter Fourteen

Walking around my apartment I realise something—I am so incredibly bored. You would think that a few days with nothing to do but relax would be a good thing, but I had enough lounging around before I finally got my job at the pool. Now, I was running out of things to entertain myself with, I have already read more books these past 72 hours than I had all year and for the first time in *too long* my apartment is completely spotless. There is only one thing I want to do and I can't. I want to call Rocco, but he isn't available as he's in meetings all day. I shake my head at how desperate I feel to hear his voice, it's 10.00am and I spoke to him before going to sleep last night, well I actually fell asleep talking to him. His voice relaxed me so much, it reminded me of the way I felt safe and cosy listening to bedtime stories when I was a little girl.

I even think about calling my mother. That's when I know I need to do something... desperately. To be entertaining the thoughts of listening to her tell me how badly I am doing, it's a cry for help. I really wish I had my bath, I could relax and soak away all my boredom. Its times like this that I miss my bath and I hate Rose a little more. I hear my mobile ringing and rush to grab it off the kitchen table, hoping that it's Rocco. It's not, and the name on the screen shocks me a little.

"Mason?"

"Thank God you're home. I need your help Makenzie." I hear the hushed words over the line.

"Why are you whispering, Mason? What's happened?" I start to feel nervous, something in his voice makes me stomach churn—something wasn't right.

"Are you busy? Please say you can come and get me, I'm at some chick's house, and I can't find my wallet." I have to try not to laugh at his apparent distress but every now and then it was refreshing to see someone like Mason get stuck in a sticky situation.

"There is only one problem with that, Mason, I don't have a car. Why don't you just call a taxi?" It's very possible he might still be a bit drunk, and if not he hasn't really thought this solution through properly.

"I can't. I don't know where my wallet is. I think she may have hidden it to stop me from leaving. She's gone all crazy. She's even locked me. In. The. House! Please, Makenzie. I have locked myself in the bathroom so I can't expect a taxi driver to save me. Get a taxi to the garage and pick up one of the loan cars. Richie will give you the keys. I will call him. *Please!*" This time I can't stop the laughter. He's locked in a bathroom and needs *me* to save him?

Payback's a bitch.

"I can't drive, Mason. You will just need to wait until she lets you go. Or maybe call one of the guys at the garage to come and get you?" I *can* drive, but at this moment he didn't need to know that. And after what I had to deal with when I left Rocco's office yesterday, he was lucky I answered in the first place.

"No, I can't tell them. I would never live it down. Shit! What the fuck am I going to do? Maybe I can fake a heart attack. No, she would call an ambulance. Shit! You need to man up dude, she is only a little woman. Please, you have to do this, I have no other options." I have tears rolling down my cheeks listening to him fight with himself, he really is desperate. If I wanted

147

something to improve my day, it's just been delivered into my lap. To listen to Mr. Game lose it over a 'date' gone wrong is just Karma working in my favour for a change.

"Calm down. I'm kidding, I can drive and I will come and rescue you, even after the shit you gave me about what happened with Rocco."

"Oh my God. You're a lifesaver, Makenzie. And I promise not to tell anyone else about what I walked in on. I will text you the address." With that, he hangs up on me. What the hell did he mean by he wouldn't tell anyone else? He's already told all the workers, the cheers we got as we left Rocco's office told me that. He wouldn't tell anyone outside of work…would he?

I arrive outside a nice little house about 40 minutes after Mason called me. I call his mobile to tell him that I am outside, but it goes straight to voicemail. Heaving a heavy sigh, I get out of the car. I run my hand over the bonnet of the car I picked up from the garage, it's a Subaru WRX. I'm pretty sure it wasn't the car I was meant to take when I got there, but there was no way I was taking any other car that was there. I wonder how pissed Mason will be when he realises I took his car, and not a loan car. I walk up to the front door of the house and knock. I can't hear any noise from inside; I stepped back to make sure I had the right house and according to Masons text it was. I knock again, louder this time hoping that whoever is inside will hear me. I hear the lock on the door slowly turning; the door swung open to show a very pretty blonde woman standing in a very revealing nightgown.

"Can I help you?" Her voice was sickly sweet but beside that, she seemed harmless. Is this really who Mason is scared of?

Before I can get any words out of my mouth, I see a figure running down the hall behind her. Mason moves around the woman's body and grabs me by the arm. I'm dragged down the garden path while she screams behind us.

"Mason, where are you going? Come back!" He falters slightly when he notices the car that I have brought.

"I'm not even gonna yell at you for this right now as long as you just open the damn door!" I would laugh if he didn't sound so more serious than I had ever witnessed before. I press the key to unlock the car as I rush around and get into the driver's seat.

Starting the car, I look at Mason, "Where are we going?"

"I don't care, just drive!" I move away from the kerb and drive. Mason lays his head back against the headrest, letting out a tortured groan, pinching the bridge of his nose between his fingers.

"Fuck. That was the booty call from hell. I swear I didn't think I was going to get out of there alive." I look over at him as I steered the car towards my apartment.

"Maybe, this is the universe's way of telling you that you need to stop being a man whore and settle down." He turns his head and smiles at me.

"Nah. It's just the universe telling me to watch out for the bat shit crazies. And if you see me start to settle down, I want you to slap me upside the head."

"Oh, Mason. That I will be more than happy to do. Not necessarily for your sake, but someone has to save that poor girl before she has to deal with Hurricane Mason."

I turn my head at the sound of his gasp; mock horror hangs on his features and in return I flash him an obnoxiously large smile. He shakes his head with a smirk, reach's out and pinches my side making me squeal. It feels great to have Mason to goof around with and for the first time I wasn't stuck staring at my four walls.

We arrived back at my apartment, with the plan to drop me off so Mason could just take his car home. Without much surprise, Mason thought the chance that the alcohol was still in his system was very high, and neither of us wanted to risk him driving home just yet. So here we sit, at my kitchen table drinking coffee. I take a large drink of my caramel mocha with a sigh. Every time I drink a mug of this now I think about Rocco and his unsweetened tea. I smile to myself, wishing again that he was here.

"I doubt very much that I'm the one putting the smile on your face just now. As much as I know you love my company, I haven't said anything remotely amazing. At least within the last few minutes" He watches me over the top of his mug as my smile widened of its own accord.

"I doubt there would be anything you could say to put this kind of smile on my face." I try hard to remove the smile from my lips, but I fail.

"Ah. So it's Mr. Cole that you are thinking about. I only know because he was walking about yesterday with the same goofy smile."

"It's not goofy! You have to be nice to me, do you not remember what I just saved you from? I can easily take you back to her." I resist the urge to stick my tongue out at him. But it's good to know that I'm not the only one who can't hide their happiness. Mason laughs at my little childish outburst. And again, I have to resist the urge to stick my tongue out. Instead, I glare at him the best I can which isn't working out the best with a huge grin on my face.

"Hey don't shoot the messenger, and for what my opinion is worth, I'm happy that he finally has a goofy smile on his face. He has been putting off living for so long, to see him happy makes an old man like me happy." He winks, but I can see beneath the silly demeanour, he was telling the truth about his happiness for Rocco. As much as he acts the joker he really does care for him.

"Was it bad? With Elle, I mean?" The smile slips from Masons's lips.

"So he told you about her?" His voice has taken on a serious tone, and if I'm not wrong there is a hint of anger in there. I haven't often seen Mason angry, but every time he speaks about Elle he seems to let some show.

"A little. Nothing big, I just know that she left him with some messed up ideas about himself."

"Yeah, that's just the tip of the iceberg, Makenzie. What she put him through, and believe me when I say, I don't think I know half of what went on, but the way she fucked with his head was beyond words. There were times that I wanted to throw a punch at her, and I would never lay my hands on a woman." I couldn't help but wonder what he had witnessed. If he felt so passionate about his hate for Elle, it must have been worse than I imagined.

"What happened to him, Mason? Can you tell me anything?" He looks at me as though trying to decide if he should share anything of Rocco's tale. With an almost unnoticeable nod of his head, he must have made his decision.

"As I say, I didn't see it all. I only saw the stuff that happened at the hospital, before and after he woke up. I swear I don't know how she didn't destroy him completely. Elle used to tell him that she couldn't believe that she was stuck with him, that he was useless, and no one would ever want him. The times I used to catch her, war would break out between us. Rocco would always stand behind her, saying she was going through a lot, that it was his fault she was like that. It used to drive me insane." A lump the size of a massive boulder formed in my throat. I can't believe that she could treat him like that, after him going through so much

151

after the accident. Instead of helping him recover she tried to destroy him.

"He keeps telling me he's broken, that he's not enough for me."

"Well, I see you've had a conversation with Elle. That's the shit she filled his head with, but I see you getting through to him. This is the first time in so long that I see him wanting more. See him wanting to spend time with someone, and not just as a friend. And it's good to finally see him get some action, well…almost. I've been telling him since she left that he needs to get out there and have some fun."

"What made her finally leave?" This is the answer that I have always wanted to know. What made her stick around to do nothing more than abuse him every way she could? If she had been that unhappy, why didn't she just leave after the accident? What was the point of staying around to be nothing more than a colossal bitch??

"He recovered." Of all the answers, I could and would have expected this wasn't even on the same page as them.

At my confused face, Mason continues.

"She didn't look like the poor girlfriend anymore. He was walking again and on the swim team. No one would ever guess what he had gone through, so she stopped looking like a saint for sticking with him. The positive attention faded away, and everyone's focus was on supporting Rocco—not her. Elle finally decided since she couldn't be the fuckin' centre of attention that there was no point sticking around. So she decided that the man she had been screwing since just before the accident could offer her more than Rocco." *Oh my God.*

"She was cheating on him while he recovered? How could she?"

"But, what's even worse," He leans in close and whispers to me like he is telling me a secret.

"He knew." *He knew?* Dozens of questions buzzed around my head that I needed a second to get them straight before I could finally speak.

"He knew? And he stayed with her?! I can't believe he put himself through that, how much he must have suffered knowing that she was with someone else, getting the one thing he couldn't give."

"Breathe, Makenzie. Just breathe. Don't give her a thought now. I don't think he has seen her since she walked out, I don't think he even knows where she is. You can't let her come between the both of you if you do then everything she worked for happens. He'll be alone. Let me ask you a question, would you let your ex come between you and Rocco?" I try to calm down. The anger that's running through my body at this moment actually shocks me a little.

"No, Carl would get nowhere near my relationship. Him or the bitch he's with." I can see the point Mason is trying to make, we both have exes and we cant let them determine our lives now, but it's hard to just ignore what Rocco has gone through at the hands of Elle. I honestly don't want to think about what I would do to her if I ever met her.

"Exactly. Just focus on the here and now. Rocco is crazy about you, anyone with eyes can see that."

"He really likes me?"

"Ah, so we are on another fishing expedition are we?" I reach out and punch Mason on the arm.

"No, you idiot. It's just nice to hear it from someone else. He has only ever mentioned it at...well at certain times."

Shut up, shut up, shut up! I need to learn when to stop speaking. I really didn't want to lead the conversation this way. If

153

there is one topic I don't want to talk about with Mason, it's what happened…or nearly happened in Rocco's office.

"I can totally imagine what times those must be," He winks at me and I feel instant heat in my cheeks. He reaches over and puts his arm around my shoulder, pulling me to his side.

"But I need to say. What I walked in on yesterday, which I never want to see every again by the way. Do you know I had to wash my eyes with soap after seeing Rocco half naked?" He fakes a shudder, and I slap him in the chest. Remembering vividly that Rocco wasn't the only one that was half naked. I close my eyes and hope that this is all a dream.

"What I caught you doing, as much as it disturbed me, it also made me really happy. I want him to be happy. He is family, and I need him to be ok. So keep doing what you're doing for my boy, whatever it is, it's working." I stand making Mason's arm drop from my shoulder, and head over to the sink to rinse my mug. I hear the words he's saying, I can understand them. But it leaves me with the one question that I am always left with. Without looking at him I ask,

"Well, if he likes me so much, then why does he run from me every time we get close?" I am so frustrated that I slam my mug on the draining board a little too hard.

"Damn it!" I yell out, feeling the hot coffee burn the skin of my hand.

"Whoa, what's wrong? Are you ok?"

"I am so *sick* of asking that question! I feel like I have asked it a million times already, and I am still no closer to getting a goddamn answer!" I hear Mason laughing behind me. I turn until I'm facing him and lean my hips back onto the sink, crossing my arms against my chest.

"I'm glad I amuse you." This time I didn't even try to keep the frustration out of my voice.

154

"For being really smart, you're really are stupid aren't you, Makenzie?" I tilt my head to the side and size him up. I am pretty sure if I started pounding on him, I could hurt him quite a bit before he managed to stop me.

"You just don't see it do you? Seriously, both of you need your fucking heads bashed together."

"God! You really can be such a douchebag sometimes! You need to make whatever point you're trying to make, I'm about a minute away from throwing your arse out. Tell me or take your unhelpful, jerky comments and leave."

"Touchy! But my point is, if he weren't with you to begin with he wouldn't be able to run away from you. He keeps coming back to you, he just can't stop himself. He is trying so hard not to want you, but he can't lie to himself."

I realise what he is saying is true. If Rocco wasn't here, trying to have, whatever this is with me, he wouldn't be able to run. I feel my shoulders relax a little as I let his words work through my mind.

"Fine. I hear what you're saying, and you have a point. But you're still a douchebag." He laughs at me again but despite my attempts to be mad—I just couldn't anymore, and joined in with a laugh.

"Yes, Makenzie. Yes I am."

Chapter Fifteen

Today's the day.

Rocco comes home tonight, and I'm so excited. I feel like a teenager going on her first date again. I haven't been able to calm my nerves all day, I think I have chosen three… no four different outfits. It isn't really a date tonight, we have planned to just go to his house and watch a movie or something. Tomorrow though, there is a big event that Rocco has invited me to go with him as his date, and I can't wait. A chance to get dressed up and to go out on his arm sounds like a dream come true. We just need to get through tonight first.

After the extra long shower I took, making sure everything was clean and…trimmed, my skin needed some hydrating lotion. Never before had I paid so much attention to making sure every little bit of my skin was covered, but I was so nervous. I wasn't going over to his house planning on anything actually happening, but I know that every time that we get close to each other, it's really hard to control the chemistry between us. I look over the clothes lying on my bed that I have chosen for tonight and smile a little.

They're sexy, in a subtle way, or at least I certainly hoped so. I have chosen my favourite blue maxi dress, it is my go-to outfit when I want to look great. It is electric blue with really big flowers all over it, matching that with a pair of silver gladiator sandals and you have a winner every time. I've let my hair dry naturally which always resulted in a small curl forming on the ends of it. I want to be the picture of relaxed tonight, so I keep my makeup to the bare minimum, a little mascara and a little bit of red gloss to give my lips a bit of a pop. Standing back and examining myself in the mirror, I'm not a big-headed person, but I think the final result looked *great*. I just prayed Rocco would agree with me.

I had paced nervously between my front door and the window that looked onto the street, waiting for Rocco to pick me up. Even though he had text to say he was on his way, there was always a little part of me that worried he wouldn't turn up. He arrived about ten minutes after his message. I had watched him turn into my street before grabbing my bag and rushing down the stairs.. He had said he didn't want me to have to get a taxi to his house so he would be there. When he pulled up at the kerb, and he was driving a sleek black Lexus LFA, I thought I might pass out when I say it. One thing that Rocco didn't know about me yet was my love of cars. Earlier in the week Masons car had fulfilled my love of fast ' boys toys' cars, but this car screamed pure sex. Slipping into the passenger seat I had to hold in a groan of appreciation, the luxury that this car had was beyond words. I never thought I would be in one of these cars since they cost more than my yearly salary, but here with Rocco I was fulfilling a dream I had always had, with a guy who I had never even dreamt possible.

The drive to Rocco's house had been relaxed. I thought that after what happened last time we were together, it might be slightly uncomfortable, but it wasn't. Chatting about his time away with work, made the distance to Rocco's house pass quickly and as we pulled up outside I was left a bit shocked by what I saw. His house is larger than I expected, it really does make my apartment look like a shoebox. Walking around the car Rocco opens my car door, taken my hand and led me into the house.

The inside is as impressive as the outside, it oozes class just like its owner. The rooms were large and open, with lots of space to move around in. It is decorated in muted tones and looks like something from a magazine, it makes me wonder if he decorated it himself. Sitting in his living room, on his large comfortable sofas, I can't tear my eyes from him as he brings a variety of food from the kitchen and places them on his coffee table. I had offered to help, but he had shooed me away, telling me to let him take care of everything. When Rocco finally sits down next to me and hands me a glass of rose wine, I take a look over all the food. There is a huge amount of it, enough to easily feed another four people.

"Did you buy enough for us to eat?" I ask, and he blushes slightly. I really do love it when he does that, it makes him look so much more innocent than I know he is. It also makes me wonder where else might be red, but thoughts like that will get me nowhere today.

"I know. I got to the shop and realised that I don't actually know what you like to eat. So I just went to the deli and bought some antipasto, hoping that you would at least like a few things I got." I reach over and place my hand on his. I have wanted to touch him since he picked me up, but other than the little kiss when he arrived at my door there's been nothing.

"It looks great, thank you." I smile at him and pick up a plate.
"So what do we have?"

Sitting back on the sofa, I don't think I will be able to move again. I have eaten so much, and I just want to sleep.

"Where do you put it all, Makenzie? I swear you ate three times more than me." I would throw a cushion at him, but I can't make myself move.

"No, I didn't. I'm a lady, I don't eat enough to keep a bird alive." A deep laugh reaches my ears, and I smile. Rolling my head to the side, I look over at his beautiful face. We have been

158

getting closer to each other, with little touches here and there. These little fleeting touches have turned me on more than most of the foreplay that I've had in the past. While eating we stuck with only discussing generic topics, nothing too deep but we had a good laugh at Mason's misfortune. I had great delight in telling Rocco everything about his 'sexcapade gone wrong'; especially the fact that Mason never did get his wallet back.

Rocco's laughter dies on his lips as we stare at each other. I don't think I will ever get bored looking at this man. He is left with that smile I love, the one that pulls more on the left side of his lips and makes his eyes sparkle.

"You really do have the most beautiful smile." *Oh God. I think I just said that out loud.*

"Shit. Did I just say that out loud?" Rocco laughs, leaning closer to me.

"I can't lie, Makenzie. You did just say that out loud." I groan making the decision to stop drinking wine.

"But its ok, because I think your smile is beautiful too." He finally closes the distance between us, placing his lips on mine. I close my eyes again, losing myself to everything except the feel of his soft lips on mine. The kiss is soft, and it makes me ache in places that desperately crave his attention. When his tongue slips into my mouth, I almost listen to the inner voices that tell me to take him. Now. He pulls back, giving me another sweet peck.

"As much as I would love to keep kissing you, we promised to talk tonight." I sigh, already missing the feeling of his mouth on mine, but I knew this talk was the most important thing right now. The whole reason we agreed to meet tonight was to clear the air, get everything out and move on. I lower my head to his shoulder.

"Yeah, I know."

"I need to tell you, Makenzie. It's the only way I can leave it behind, and the only way you will be able to decide if you want to be with me."

"Rocco, I don't need to know about your past to know I want to be with you. I would love to know what is keeping you from me, so maybe I can help you move past it. But know that I like the man you are now, no matter what. I'm hoping that one of the times I tell him this, he will actually hear me.

His past had shaped him, but it didn't define him.

"I hope you still feel that way once you know." He takes a deep breath, almost as if he trying to steel himself for what he is going to dive into. I try to mentally prepare myself, I know it's going to be awful; the things that Mason has told me made me want to cry, and I have a feeling that they are a drop in the ocean compared to what is about to come out of Rocco's mouth.

"I met Elle when I first bought the garage, it wasn't a shop at the time but I had my plan all set out with Mason. She appeared in my life like the sun on a cloudy day, she just brightened everything. She helped break through all the stress I was dealing with, with all the work going on. I think she was the one who actually swept me off my feet. Mason knew of her reputation and told me not to get too serious, but I didn't listen, in fact, I did the opposite. We moved so fast, now I can see that she was always pushing for the next step, but at the time I thought it all felt right. When the garage was finally finished, it took off better than either Mason, or I could have dreamed. We were the only custom bike shop in the area, so we were always busy, once our name got out we had people travelling long distances to use us. It was the ultimate dream come true." He looks genuinely happy. It was obviously they had worked so hard to make his business the success that it is now.

"It wasn't long after the big money starting coming in that Elle started to complain about not seeing enough of me, and no matter how much extra time I tried to give her, she was never happy. I soon realised that the thing that made her the happiest was when I was buying her things. Clothes, jewellery, holidays, you name it—I bought it. I should have seen the warning signs then, but I was just happy to have someone by my side. The day I went for a ride to clear my head was the day I found out that she was cheating on me." I can't sit next to him and not touch him anymore. I need to have some sort of contact, so I reach out and entwine my fingers with his, hoping to give him some of my strength.

"I'm sorry, Rocco. I know what it's like to have someone cheat on you. There is nothing more humiliating than that." He looks at me with an expression of pain.

"That's the thing, Makenzie. I needed to clear my head because I wasn't upset that she was cheating, I was relieved." Wow. Not the experience I had when I found out about Carl and the devil woman.

"That's why I needed to get away, to think. And well, you know what happened when I was out. I don't even know if I had made a decision about what I was going to do, but when I woke up it didn't matter. When I opened my eyes in the hospital, I grabbed onto Elle with both hands and refused to let go. I needed her to be with me and no matter what she seemed to do, I was always willing to take it." Even though I knew I wouldn't like the answer to my next question, I needed to ask it.

"What did she do to you, Rocco?" He uses the hand that I'm not holding, to scrub through his hair making it stick up slightly.

"Wow. I never thought I would have to relive this again." He lets out a huge breath. I move closer to him on the sofa, needing as little distance between us as possible.

161

"Some things were worse than others. If she was in a good mood then, there was a good chance the only thing, she would do was ignore me. Other times, the times she would get angry, they were the times I wished I had my body back so I could have left. She spent the whole time in the hospital telling me how useless I was, how no woman would ever want my broken body. When you hear something enough, you start to believe it."

"I think I remember hearing those words somewhere before." I squeeze his hand, trying to make him feel better.

"Ha, yeah. Well, what can I say? When you are told something every day for a long time, you kinda start to believe it. So it might take me a little while to leave all that self-doubt behind, and believe what you are trying to say." Dropping my hand, Rocco leans forward and refills my wine glass, picking it up and handing it to me.

"Am I going to need this?" He gives a chuckle, but it doesn't, even in the slightest, sound happy.

"I will let you decide. Do you want me to continue?" I nod my head at him, taking a drink of wine to cover the fact that I don't trust my voice.

"It started off just verbal. She wanted me to know how much she was suffering, how much she was doing to help me; which is actually funny as she never once took me to my physical therapy appointments. Once I got released from the hospital it got worse. She was living with me by this point, and there was nowhere I could go. I was still in a wheelchair when I first came home. It was before I started swimming, and I hardly had any strength and honestly I needed a lot of help. There were times I was stuck in bed while she went out with her lover."

The one thing I didn't want to do was show any emotion during the story that Rocco was telling me, because I knew how important it was for him to get everything out. It was easier said than done as I could feel the tears building in my eyes. The lump in my throat is getting hard to swallow around, taking a shaky breath I try to calm my nerves. Rocco must have noticed my reaction, letting me see how bad of a job I'm doing of covering it. He takes the glass from my hand and places them back on the table. Sitting back, he pulls me into him, turning me, so my back is sitting against his chest; wrapping his arms around me, holding me tight. It is easier talking to him like this, having his warmth against me, and not having to look into his eyes.

"Did she ever hurt you? Physically, I mean."

"A few times, only one time pretty bad. She'd been out with Jamie, that's the guy she left me for, and she left me in bed to take care of myself. It was a bad day and the pain I was suffering made it difficult for me to move. I remember she was gone for hours, it had gotten dark outside, and I was really hungry. I would have called Mason but if she had come home to him being there she wouldn't be happy. They didn't exactly get on." I laugh thinking that must be the understatement of the year. I know how much Mason hates her, even now.

"He may have mentioned his love for her, just a little."

"Yeah, Mason doesn't have any problem letting people know he hates her, but I can't blame him. I think he always knew there was more going on than I told him, especially after getting hurt that night." I turn my nose into his neck, breathing in his scent.

"What happened?" I keep cuddled into his neck, wanting to stay as close as possible to him. He places a kiss to my head before he answers me.

"I wasn't just hungry, I also needed to go to the bathroom, I held on as long as I could, I even tried to move myself but I just couldn't. By the time, she came home it was too late." He stops talking, and I feel his arms tighten around me. I stay quiet,

163

knowing it must be taking a lot for him to admit all this. When he speaks again his voice is soft.

"She was so mad. All I remember is her screaming at me, calling me names. She picked up a vase from the dressing table and threw it at me. Lucky for me, her aim wasn't great and it hit the wall instead of me. She kept screaming about how she would have to clean up the mess, and how I never thought of anyone but myself. She climbed onto the bed and pushed me to the side so she could remove the sheet, but she pushed too hard and I fell onto the floor. I landed awkwardly and the pain that shot through my spine was the worst thing I had ever felt." I feel Rocco's tears drip from his face down onto mine. I pull away and look at him. The pain I see in his eyes as he relives this moment steals my breath. I have never seen someone look so vulnerable. I cup his face in my hands, using my thumbs to wipe the tears from his cheeks. I lean forward and gently kiss him.

"Don't tell me anymore. I don't need to know. It's done, she can't hurt you anymore. I have you now and I won't let you fall." I place little kisses to his face, starting at his eyes, kissing his tears away. Then downs his cheeks, across his strong jaw and back up to his lips.

"I have you." I whisper. I feel his sigh against my lips as he places his forehead against mine.

"Stay with me tonight, Makenzie. I just want to hold you." I nod slightly against his head, feeling my heart beating hard in my chest.

"Anything you need, Rocco. Anything."

Rocco's bedroom fits really well with the rest of the house. It's a large bedroom, my whole apartment would probably fit into this one room, with light walls and dark furniture. It seems to be the design that Rocco likes the most. Even his office has the dark furniture. I'm lying in the biggest bed I think I have ever seen, but the fact I'm lying in Rocco's arm I wouldn't care if I was lying on the floor. He has his arms wrapped around me tightly, like he doesn't want me to be an inch away from him. Between all the food I have eaten and the wine I have drunk I can feel myself drifting off to sleep. I am so relaxed in his arms, I could spend my life here and never want to leave.

"Why do you like me, Makenzie?" His whispered voice breaks through my foggy mind.

"Your body, it's hot." I feel his laughter against my back and it makes me smile.

"Everything, Rocco. I like everything about you. You're a great friend, loyal, hardworking and as I mentioned, hot as hell." I can hear the slur in my voice, I know it won't be long until I'm asleep. He places kisses along my neck and shoulders.

"That all sounds good. Sleep now pretty lady, it's late." With a final kiss I allow sleep to take me, but just before I drifted into darkness I hear Rocco whispering against my ear.

"You better watch out, Makenzie. I think I could easily fall in love with you."

Chapter Sixteen

"Damn, woman. You scrub up well." I'm standing just inside the door at Rocco's work function. The room is full of people, dressed in their Sunday best. Everywhere you look women are stunning in their expensive and beautiful cocktail dresses, and the men all looked rather handsome in their tuxedos. But by far the most handsome guy in the room is stood next to me. When I first saw Rocco at my door, I was lost for words. I just stood and stared, which was funny as he was doing the same to me. It took us both several minutes to finally speak, and then Rocco refused to come into my apartment claiming that if he did we wouldn't make it to the function.

The second best looking man in the room is Mason. He looks almost as good as Rocco does in his tuxedo, but no one will ever look as good as the man here with me.

I look down at what I'm wearing and smile to myself. I had bought this dress just before I left Carl, and now I was happy to finally have somewhere to wear it. Its an ankle length red silk gown; it's skin tight and makes me feel sexy as hell. One of the things about this dress is that I can't wear underwear with it. It's making me feel daring, but also a little exposed. I have never been the type of person with the confidence to go without panties, but knowing that I can maybe shock Rocco with this little bit of information later gives me the push I needed to do it.

"Thank you, Mason. You don't look so bad yourself." I laugh as he gives me a little pirouette.

"Save a dance for me sexy, and if I don't get lucky Rocco better watch out, because I'm taking you home." He walks away with a wink to Rocco. Rocco slips his arm around my waist and whispers in my ear.

"I better not let you out of my sight tonight, Mason might steal you." Turning to face him, I press a kiss to his lips.

"Never gonna happen." The smile he gives me is the one that gets me every time. The one that lit up his whole face and honestly, the sight brightened my soul.

Rocco has kept good on his word, and I haven't been more than a couple of steps away from him all night. He's made sure that he is always connected to me in some way, a hand on my lower back or our fingers laced together. My confidence has steadily grown as we walk around and meet people, and I'm able to connect to everyone that I've met so far. Everyone that I'm introduced to seems really nice; they have all been friendly and showed genuine interest in getting to know me. Rocco seems to flourish in this situation, he is a very social person and truly gives people his full attention and even without them saying anything, I know it means a lot. I'm not surprised that his business does so well, if this is the person that goes into all those meetings he must be very skilled at charming them—he definitely charmed me.

After a few hours, my heels are seriously killing my feet so when Rocco suggested I sit down—I didn't argue. He made sure I had a drink before excusing himself to chat with a group of business partners. I don't mind sitting down, it gives me a chance to people watch and observe what everyone was up to. I can see Mason trying to work his charms on a redhead at the other side of the dance floor. He looks like he's making progress with all the hair flicking and arm touching she is doing. Mason looks around, and the smile on his face dies and he freezes. I look in the direction he is staring, but I can't see anything that

167

seems out of place. There is a group of guys chatting and a female hanging onto the arm of one the guys. I look back to Mason, and he notices me looking at him. He gives me a little nod and goes back to chatting to the redhead. I look back at the group, but they're all still talking, and it makes me wonder if maybe Mason has spent the night with the female. It really wouldn't surprise me, I make a mental note to ask him about it later. This is the type of information that I can use to my advantage, getting to tease him for a change.

Strong arms grab me around the waist, and a kiss is placed to my shoulder.

"Would you like to dance, pretty lady?" That deep voice in my ear makes the butterflies in my belly appear. I wonder if there will ever be a time when he doesn't make them flutter every time he's near. I sit there trying to be calm as I say over my shoulder.

"I don't know, my date may get jealous." I am rewarded with a bite on my neck. God, does this man know what he does to me?

"Move your arse, hot stuff." He grabs my hand as he moves away from me towards the dance floor. I pretend to myself that I am following him as I have no option, but I know it's not that, I am going to be in his arms again, and there is nowhere else I would rather be.

"You're very demanding, Mr. Cole."

"Only with you." He finishes that with a kiss. I think it was meant to be a sweet brush of his lips, but soon it deepens. Sparks fly around my body as his tongue meets mine, brushing over it gently before he sucks it into his mouth. Pulling his body closer to me like we are all alone, I don't even care who is watching us. I will never get enough of this man.

"Do I really need to hose you two down? Every time I turn around you are trying to have sex." What is it with Mason

168

constantly stopping my pleasure? I groan when Rocco's lips pull back from mine.

"What do you want now cock block?" I say in a voice that I hope sounds angry, but I don't think I pull it off. I feel Rocco's chest going up and down against mine as he laughs.

"Oh, someone has her talons out tonight." Mason says with a laugh. I love the fact we can tease each other without anybody's feelings being hurt.

"But I need to speak to your man, I will only keep him a minute. Promise."

"Fine. I should go freshen up my make-up anyway." I turn back to Rocco and place a chaste kiss against his lips.

"I won't be long."

I come back from the bathroom and look around the room for Rocco. I'm heading towards the bar to see if maybe he is waiting there for me. I see Mason standing to the side of the bar, and he's glaring again. I thought Rocco was with him? I look about again, starting to wonder exactly where Rocco is; the way Mason is looking is making me feel uneasy. He looks so angry, and I have never seen Mason angry before, he finds the laughter in any situation. I follow his stare again, and he is looking at the same woman as earlier, the difference this time is that she isn't standing with the man from before. She is talking to Rocco, and he doesn't look happy. She has a sneer on her face that I don't understand, and Rocco has lost that spark of joy that he had when I left a few minutes ago. I can't figure out what is going on; we haven't spoken to this woman tonight, so I don't even know who she is. Rocco looks up from the conversation and our eyes meet, and my heart breaks. It is the same look that he had last night when we were talking about...then it hits me.

This is Elle.

The woman that broke his soul is now standing in front of him saying, god only knows. I am just about to move when Rocco closes his eyes and his chin drops to his chest. I can only imagine the pain that he is going through and the protective instinct within me wants to run to him, slap her silly and pull him into my arms. He shakes his head at something she says, and her smile gets even bigger. Lifting his head he looks back at me, and I can see the unshed tears in his eyes. Then he does the thing that I thought we were passed, the one thing I thought he wouldn't ever do again. He walks away. I can tell by the look on his face that he isn't just going somewhere to compose himself, he is leaving the function, leaving me.

I start to rush after him when a laugh reaches my ears. I turn around and see Elle laugh as she watches Rocco walk away with a look of defeat radiating from his slumped shoulders. I have heard people talking about the red mist that takes over when they are angry, but I never believed it. Until now. The only sound that I can hear is her bitchy laughter, all other noise has disappeared. My focus is fully on the smile that the bitch is wearing, the one that I want to wipe from her face. I can't control my body, it's like someone else has taken control. Closing the distance between us quickly, all my thoughts are on finding out what she did to him. Standing in front of Elle, watching the look of triumph in her eyes, I react before any thought can enter my mind. My hand connects with her cheek, with enough power to snap her head to the side. Elle turns her head back to me with her eyes wide, and she has lost the smile that had been on her lips.

"You're a bitch! What did you say to him? What shit did you tell him to mess with his mind this time?" I don't even notice the crowd that has gathered around us. All I can focus on is the woman in front of me that, by now, must have worked out who I am. Her hand has dropped, and she is smiling again.

"Ah, so you're the one who tried to put the smile back on Rocco's face? I wondered why he looked so happy. But don't you worry your pretty little head, I reminded him exactly who he is." I lunge for her, but before I can make contact a strong pair of arms wrap around me, pulling me backwards.

"Mason! Let me go, I will do to her what you have always wanted to do." I hear him laugh behind me, but he doesn't loosen his hold on me.

"As much as I would love to see you beat her down, Makenzie, she isn't worth it."

He whispers into my ear.

"He needs you, Makenzie. Don't let your hate for her take you away from him; we need to find him." I stop fighting against his hold.

He's right, at this time she isn't worth my time. She's worth nothing but the man that stole my heart is. I need to go to Rocco, before he believes all her words again. I look her up and down with disgust filling my expression.

"Yeah, Mason. You're right. She isn't worth anyone's time." I walk away from her with my head held high. Leaving behind the woman that broke the man I love.

Love? Do I love Rocco? I really think I do. Mason catches up with me and throws his arm around my shoulder.

"Come on, Rocky. Let's go and get your man."

Chapter Seventeen

Rushing from the hotel that the function is held, my heart drops when I notice that Rocco's car is gone from where he parked it. He really did leave. I check my phone to see if he had sent me a message, but there's nothing. He has disappeared.

"Where would he go, Mason?" We are moving quickly towards his car. We both know it's important to find Rocco, to find out what Elle has said to him. I'm scared that she's finally broken him, that I won't ever get my Rocco back. The look he had in his eyes as he left scared me, I had never seen him look so shattered, not even when he was reliving the past.

"I'm not sure. Maybe we should start with the obvious places first. Let's try the garage since it's the closest, and then try his place." Mason is trying to seem calm, but I can see the worry in his eyes. I might lose the man I love, but Mason may lose his best friend.

We had checked the garage, but we hadn't found Rocco. We are now driving towards his house, I have all my hopes pinned on him being there. I don't know if my nerves will last if we have to try and think of another place that he might be. The only other place I can think of is the pool, but I don't want to think about having to go there. The drive has been quiet, there is nothing to talk about and I think that Mason is stuck in his head, just as much as I am. I keep thinking that I should ask him if he is ok, but his hands gripping the steering wheel show me that he is barely holding onto his anger. So I leave him to his thoughts, hoping that he can settle the emotions that he is feeling.

Pulling into Rocco's street, I release the breath that I think I have been holding since the hotel. His car is in his driveway. Mason pulls to a stop behind it but doesn't turn off the engine. I turn to look at him.

"Are you not coming in?"

"No, Makenzie. I think this is something that only you can help with. I can only imagine the things she said to him, about being broken and useless. You are the only one that can prove to him that's she's wrong." I feel tears building behind my eyes. This Mason right in front of me is the one that I love. The one with a huge heart, the one that would do anything for someone he loves. I reach over and squeeze his hand.

"Thank you. I will text you when I can." Leaning over he gives me a small kiss on my cheek.

"Take care of my boy." I open the car door and leave, before I lose the battle to hold back my tears.

"Will you stop running away from me, Rocco." He turns to looks at me, and I can see his eyes are still riddled with that gut wrenching pain. I have finally got him to open his front door. I had stood for a while after Mason left, just trying to get Rocco to open it. He hadn't said anything when I had started to knock, but I knew he was there, I swear I felt like I could feel his pain through the door. When I had threatened to call the police to come and check on him, he had finally relented and opened it. The vision that met me when the door opened wasn't one that I will ever forget. He looked like he was breaking from the inside out.

"Rocco, please. Will you tell me what happened?" His head falls in defeat as he leans back against the wall.

For a few unbearable moments of silence, I felt how strongly her words had affected his battered soul. My stomach twisted, and something told me that I was losing him.

"I can't do this, Makenzie. I thought I could, but I can't be the man you want. The man you need." I watch him closely wondering exactly what had happened. Why were we back to this again? I thought we had gotten past his disbelief that I want him. I walk over to him, standing as close to him as I can without actually touching him.

"Look at me, Rocco." He doesn't raise his head, instead he lowers himself down the wall until he is sitting on the floor, placing his head in his hands. He is breaking in front of me, and I need to stop him, to save him. Dropping to my knees next to him, I place my hand on his chin I lift it until I can see his beautiful, pain filled eyes.

"Tell me what happened." I say gently, just above a whisper.

"The woman you saw me talking to, that was Elle."

"Yeah, I worked that out. And I don't know what she said, and I really don't care. You can't let her get under your skin. You are so much better than she is. You need to see all the people that are around you Rocco. We love you." I try to think of another way to show him the type of man he is. That he is the only person that I want. It's not the way I want to tell him, but I think he needs to know. I take a deep breath and let out the words that I hope will show him what he means to me.

"I love you, Rocco." I manage on barely a whisper. Even though I only admitted it to myself earlier in the evening, right now, with his courage and confidence dwindling he needs to know my feelings. He looks into my eyes, and I know he's struggling with it, he wants to believe me but her voice just won't let him. I move my face closer to him, placing my lips next to his ear and whisper,

"I love you, Rocco." He lets out a pained breath. It sounds like it has been ripped from the bottom of his soul. I repeat the words to him.

"I love you, Rocco." I place a kiss under his ear, under my lips I can feel his body shudder. If he won't believe my words then he will have to believe my actions. I will not leave this house until he fully understands and believes the love I have for him. I let my lips follow the curve of his jaw, the feel of his slight stubble on my lips sends a surge of electricity through my body.

I need this man, more than he will possibly ever know. Moving towards his lips, I stop and look at him. He has his eyes closed, I wonder if he wants me to stop. I don't want to. He opens his eyes and looks straight at me. I'm sure he can see straight into me, and I wonder if my eyes reflect the heat that's in his.

"Don't stop. Please." I move to close the small distance between us, my lips brushing over his gently, letting him back away if he wants. Instead of backing away like I thought he might, he puts his hand to the back of my neck, pulling me closer. The heat in the kiss increases, the gentleness is replaced by a desperation that I can feel flowing from Rocco to me. Feeling his hand tangle in my hair, I move my body closer to him, until I feel my breasts rub against his chest.

My lungs start to burn with the need to breathe, but I don't want to lose the contact with his searing lips. I'm afraid if I pull away from him he will stop and run like he always does. I let a small gasp out when I pull back from him, and I can finally breathe. I place kisses on his cheek. He lowers his knees, extending his legs out in front of him. I don't hesitate to crawl into his lap, straddling his legs. The split on my dress opens fully on my left side, allowing me to sit comfortably. It also leaves my left leg completely bare right up to the top of the thigh. He moves the hand that isn't holding my neck down to hold my hip, gently pulling me closer into him. I grind my hips, feeling his erection straining inside his tuxedo trousers. Listening to the groan he lets out gives me confidence to keep going, maybe I'm getting through to him just how much I want him.

His lips find my neck, causing goose bumps all over my body. He can get such a huge reaction from me by doing so little. He finds that spot where my neck joins my shoulder and bites it gently, before soothing it with his tongue. He pulls on my hair bringing my head back to give his mouth full access to my neck, moving lower he nips along my collarbone. I noticed that my hands have moved from his hair and are now grabbing onto the front of his shirt, and I don't remember moving them there. He lets me raise my head again, and our lips meet, our tongues tangle and our hips pulse together.

We touch from head to toe, but I crave to touch him more, to feel him over every part of my body at once. With his hands and his lips. Closing my eyes, I grind my hips harder into him, I can feel him close to my core and the few layers that separate us are driving me insane, I just want him inside me. I am concentrating so hard on the feel of his erection against me that I am surprised when I feel the strap of my dress fall from my shoulder. I open my eyes and see that Rocco has slid it down; he pulls it further until my breast is uncovered and naked in front of him. He uses his thumb to rub over my very erect nipple, the friction causing my belly muscle to tense. This in turn causes the fire in my core to get bigger. I want Rocco to hurry up and take me, but I also want this to never end. I want to savour every moment.

His lips move down to my breast, kissing from the top until he has my nipple in his mouth. The heat from his mouth is like lava on me, I feel like he is marking them with his tongue. He removes my other strap as he continues to lavish my nipple with his mouth, giving it more attention that it has ever had. My breasts feel heavy with the arousal he has flooding through my body. He moves his mouth to my other breast giving it the same attention. The coolness of the hallway attacks my wet nipple making me shudder. Rocco lifts his head to look at me.

"Are you ok?" He asks in a husky voice. I pull on his bowtie that was lying loose around his neck, throwing it to the floor.

"I'm better than ok." I lean forward again, capturing his lips while I start to undo his buttons on his shirt. I nibble his lips and then sooth them with my tongue. His breathing has increased almost to the point of gasping, and when I run my hands inside his open shirt feeling his beautifully carved abs he lets out a groan.

"Are you ok?" I ask him with a smile.

"I'm better than ok." He replies with a laugh.

"Can I make a suggestion?" He asks as he continues to palm my breasts. The feeling is amazing, and I'm trying so hard to concentrate on what he's saying to me. His pam is slightly calloused, and these are rubbing over my nipple.

"If you keep doing that, then no. You feel so amazing." I lean forward and kiss him again. I can't keep my lips off him. He pushes me back slightly, only far enough that our lips part.

"Amazing. But when I'm with you for the first time, I don't want it to be on my hall floor. Can we, please move before I get too carried away to care?"

"And you promise if we stop you won't run away from me?" I smile at him, so he knows I am teasing him, and I am a little. There is a part of me though that is scared that he will run, and I want him to stop running now I have him exactly where I want him.

"Makenzie, I swear that there is nothing in this world that would make you leave my bed tonight." Placing a gentle kiss on my lips he pushes me up to my feet, I grab his hand and help him off the floor. Not dropping my hand he pulls me in the direction of his bedroom.

It feels like forever since we were in here last, not just since last night. Rocco drops my hand as he goes to close the curtains. I walk over to look at the selection of photograph's that line his wall. I had noticed them last night but hadn't paid much attention. The photos are all black and white scenic pictures, there are a few were of the ocean with big waves crashing onto the shore. They are breathtaking. There are another few of city skylines, but there was no way I could name the cities. Rocco wraps his arms around my waist and rests his chin on my shoulder as I stand there looking at them.

"These are beautiful, Rocco. I have never seen anything like them before."

"My brother Noah took them. It's just a hobby. I think he should take it up professionally, but he won't listen to me."

"I agree. He's wasting an amazing talent." They really are eye catching, and even though they are black and white they seem to have so much life in them.

"As much as I love my brother, I think I would rather talk about how I can get you back into that big bed over there." He whispers into my ear. Little does he know that he really doesn't have to do much at all, he would never have to do much. I've been drawn to him since I met him, even my body knew before my brain did that he was it. He is the one.

"Rocco, all you need to do is ask." I turn in his arms to face him, I don't think I will ever get tired of looking at his beautiful face.

"Makenzie," he whispers against my lips, his breath warm against me. I am glad that he is holding me still, or I would have been in a puddle on the floor.

"Will you, please let me make love to you?"

"Oh God, Rocco." I think I actually swoon, but he is there to catch me again. I realize that he has been there catching me for a while now, I just haven't noticed before. Once I know that my legs can take my weight again, I step back from his body. I can feel his eyes all over me, the heat from them almost burning my skin as they move over me. The look that Rocco is giving me is pure desire, he looks as though I'm the most beautiful thing he has ever seen. It gives me confidence in what I'm about to do. I let the straps of my dress fall from my shoulders, swaying my body slightly the dress is quickly lying around my ankles. Standing completely naked in from of him, nowhere to hide. I feel relaxed and comfortable standing there, and I know I don't want to hide anything from him.

"You are the most beautiful woman I have ever seen." His eyes haven't made it back up to my face yet. Moving forward I stand right in front of him, close enough to feel his heat, to smell him, but not close enough that we are touching. I reach out and push his shirt from his shoulders. Now it's my turn to take in his body, he honestly looks like he is sculpted by a world-renowned artist. I give in to the temptation that is standing before me and run my hand down his abdomen.

The muscles tremble under my touch, making them tight. Not allowing my hands to stop their downward decent on his body I run my fingers along the waistband of his trousers. Undoing the button and lowering the zip, I push his trousers down over his hips. His eyes haven't left mine since I moved closer to him, his breathing is getting quicker and matches mine now. Both of us are just standing there, just staring at each other but not touching. I break eye contact, starting to feel exposed, and my nerves are starting to show through.

Rocco growls before he grabs me, hands tangling in my hair tilting my head back as his lip's slam against mine. We move backwards across his room until the back of my legs hit his bed, and I tumble onto it with Rocco still attached to me. His kisses consume me with so much passion and need. I try to be equal in what I give him back, but there is no mistaking who is now in control. He moves us further up the bed, and never once does his lips leave me.

My lips. My neck. My breasts. The heat of my body is intense, the wetness between my legs can no longer be hidden, and I'm scared that I might orgasm before he actually gets inside me.

"Rocco. Oh God, Rocco. You're going to have to hurry up. I can't take anymore." He stands at the bottom of the bed, I prop myself up on my elbows and watch as he finally, yes lord finally, removes his boxer shorts. My mouth goes dry looking at him. My core tightens and I'm in real danger of that orgasm, just imaging him inside me. I have never seen a man look as perfect as he does, he is truly every woman's dream come true. But in the midst of my admiration he suddenly stopped, turned and alarm strikes as I watched him walk away from me.

"Rocco?" He must have heard the panic in my voice because even I felt the hysteria coursing through me. He can't leave me this way.

"Beautiful, I will be back in one minute." I watch as he goes through the door leaving his room, he reappears less than a minute later holding a little square foil packet in his raised fingers.

"We can't get very far without this." He is wearing that smile that makes my heart beat faster. The one of pure joy.

"True, but maybe you should grab more than one." I wink at him as I watch him start to crawl up the bed towards me. His lips graze over my skin as he moves higher, everywhere he touches gets me hotter and less patient.

"Rocco, I love you," I kiss him on the lips.

"But I swear, if you don't hurry up I am going to tie you to this bed and have my wicked way with you." This actually makes him laugh. Maybe he thinks I'm joking?

"As fun as that sounds, maybe next time." He lowers his body onto mine. It's the first time I have felt him naked against me, and I am sure this is what heaven feels like. He is hard all over but warm and gentle. I can feel his erection settling between my legs, moving slightly to create friction on my clit. My eyes roll in my head. He really is trying to kill me. My hands are touching everywhere I can, and I am getting myself worked up into a heated mess. Rocco groans when I tilt my hips up into him.

"I want this to last so long for you, Makenzie. But I can't. I need to have you now. I'm sorry." Rocco pants these words in between grinding into me.

"Don't make me wait." I plead with him, not ashamed to be begging. He leans back from me, putting the condom on. Propping himself over me on this arms, he reaches down and runs his fingers along me. I gasp at his touch.

"You are so wet. Are you ready for me?" I try to answer him, but he pushes two fingers into me stealing all my thoughts. Pumping them in and out of me slowly, gradually building up speed as I struggle to keep my hips on the bed. It takes all the control I have to just lie there and enjoy the moment. I moan as he slips his fingers back into my body, and it seems to break the last portion of control Rocco has. He leans down over my body again and kisses me, little sweet kisses, as his tongue tastes my mouth.

I feel the heat from his erection as he places it at my opening. I want to push forward, I want him to slam into me, to fill me. He gently pushes into me. I feel the thickness of him spread my muscles, stretching to almost the point of pain, pain that is still pleasure. I dig my nails into the skin on his back making him grunt. I can't stop it, the feeling is just so intense. Soon he is fully filling me, touching deep inside. He stays still, and I just want him, no I need him to move.

"Rocco. Please move." His head falls against mine, and he whispers.

"Give me a minute, Makenzie. Please. It's been so long, and you feel so good. I'm trying to get control." I feel happy that I am making him feel so good, but he is making me go insane. I move my hips under his, making him move out of me slightly. Rocco must gain some control, and he pulls out of me. My muscles clench as he leaves, missing him already. He pushes back into me gently, before pulling out again. It feels like I have waited my entire life for this moment, nothing that I have been with before compares to this, but I need it harder, faster. I place my hands on Rocco's cheeks and look him in the eyes.

"Harder." Pulling out of me, he thrusts back in. Hard. Little lights start going off behind my eyes as he continues his hard thrusting, his pace getting faster. I can feel my muscles start to tighten in my stomach, the pressure at my core getting ready to explode.

"Oh God, Rocco. Yes. Harder!" I scream as he continues to pound into me. He starts to lose his rhythm, his thrusting getting erratic. He thickens inside me, and it is that that finally sends me over the edge. I grip onto his biceps and my back arches off the bed, my inner muscles grabbing him as I scream his name. It only takes a few more thrusts, and Rocco is joining me in pleasure, groaning my name into my neck.

We both lie there for a few minutes, trying to catch our breath. I can't believe how amazing being with him is. My body still feels like little fireworks are going off throughout it. I run my hands up and down Rocco's back, feeling his scars under my fingertips, and smiling at myself. I can't believe I'm finally holding this man in my arms, every imperfect but perfect inch of him. He raises his head from my shoulder, leaning on his arm he uses the other to push some hair from my forehead. He leans forward and gives me a gentle kiss on my lips.

"That was...wow. That was just wow." He says to me, his voice sounding a little rough.

"Yeah. Wow is a good word for it. I have waited a long time for that to happen with you, Rocco."

"I'm sorry." I look at him with a glare.

"I swear Rocco, if you apologise for this happening before you ru..." My words are cut off as his lip's land on mine, kissing them away.

"I mean, I'm sorry it took so long to do this. That I kept running away. I should have claimed you as my girl a long time ago." He says placing small kisses over my cheeks.

"I have been your girl for a while now, Rocco. I think the first time I saw you I started to fall for you. And every time I saw you after the park I tried to forget you, especially when you kept pushing me away. But now you're stuck with me, for, however, long you want me." I need to let him know I'm his. I'm not going anywhere.

"Is forever ok?" He whispers.

"We can start with forever and then play it by ear." He laughs at my answer, I know it's cheesy, but I just don't care. It's the way I feel. I have lost my heart to this man, and I want to be his forever. I want to be his wife and give him the family that he wants. I want all my good times to be with him, and him to hold me through all my bad times. I want to be his strength, his friend, his lover and his life. I can't imagine being anywhere but with

183

him. I reach up and kiss him gently on the lips, the feeling of love and security embracing me while I lie in his arms. This is it for me, he really does have my heart. Rocco is looking at me, but I can't make out the look on his face, I think he looks happy.

"Rocco, are you ok?"

"I need to tell you something. And I should have told you before now but it was never the right time." My heart rate increases and I can feel it beat against my ribcage in panic.

"Makenzie. I have been broken for so long, that I forgot what it feels like to be whole. To feel my heart beating without pain and doubt rushing through it. To know that there is someone out there willing to love me, accept all my scars. You have made me realize what I've been missing this whole time." My heart rate is still fast but for a different reason this time.

And then he says the words that I want to hear, the ones that make my heart skip a beat.

The ones that will make life never be the same again.

The ones that I have wanted to hear for so long now.

"I love you, Makenzie."

Epilogue

Rocco ~ Eight months later.

This is the biggest swim race of the year. I need to try and focus and get my head on straight, but I know that this isn't going to happen anytime soon when my eyes move over to the spectator's area looking for her. Makenzie. My girl. I still can't believe that I can call her that. My eyes land on her, and my breath gets stuck in my chest again. I don't think there will ever be a time when she doesn't take my breath away. She is so beautiful. I have never known a girl like her before. Her love and compassion have left me in awe of her. If there was ever an example of beauty on the inside as well as the outside, it is Makenzie. I smile to myself as I watch her talk to Matt. She is on the pool side of the dividing glass, and I know what a big step it is for her after everything. My mind flashes back to the moment I nearly lost her, it is officially the scariest moment of my life.

Nothing I have been through compares to it.

But she's here, and she is working through her own demons, and I will be here to help her like she helped me. With my eyes wandering over her body I see that she is wearing my favourite dress again, she calls it my lucky dress and wears it at all my races. The dress ties around her neck, leaving her back completely bare, and I know that's why I love it, because it shows her tattoo. The one she got in memory of her sister. She may not have physical scars like me but this tattoo is a reminder that she still bears internal scars, the weight of her past is still with her.

This is something I can understand. My tattoo is there to hide the scars on my body, trying to pretend that they aren't there. I just didn't know until I met her that it was my internal scars that I was letting take over my life.

We have been together now for eight months and so much has happened. We are living together, and I know when I win this race today, I am getting down on one knee and asking her to be my wife. I think back to the first time I saw her, sitting on that park bench. I remember the feeling I got in my gut when I heard her shout out, there was no way I could just walk past, I needed to see who owned that voice. When she jumped up and turned, I swear my heart skipped a beat. I know how corny that sounds, but it really did. That was the day I thought that maybe I could feel again.

I start to stretch out my body, but my eyes never leave her. I watch as Mason walks over to her, and she hits him on the chest. I can only imagine what he has said to her, he's lucky he's my friend and I'm not the jealous type. There are only so many times someone should ever hear their best friend proposition your girlfriend, but that is just Mason. There is something happening with him lately, and I need to find out what. He seems...different. I can't quite put my finger on it. We'll go out and have a drink after my brother, Noah arrives tonight. He's flying in for my proposal tonight, and he's going to stay on for a little while.

Makenzie turns and looks at me. Maybe she can feel me staring, again. Whenever we are in the same room, my eyes are drawn to her. I just want to be touching her all the time. I walk about with a permanent hard on, my body can't seem to have enough of her. She jokes that it's trying to make up for the year I went without, but she's wrong. It's her. Just pure and simply her.

She gives me that smile she always gives me when she is thinking naughty thoughts, and damn if my body doesn't start reacting to it. My cock starts to harden, knowing what usually happens after I get that smile. Shit! I look away as quickly as I can hoping it's not too late to get back under control, standing in front of all these people wearing just skin-tight tiny swim trunks is not a good thing. Nope, not a good thing at all. A loud laugh reaches me, and I look towards it. Mason has obviously worked out what has happened, and he finds it extremely amusing. His laughter is loud through the quiet pool area, and people are starting to look. I really wish he would stop, before I have to go over and smack him. On the upside, his laughing has made me lose the semi I had been sporting in my trunks.

The whistle sounds, and it's time for me to go to the start for my race. I stand at the side of the pool waiting on the other swimmers to get into place, but I can't resist looking over to Makenzie one last time. And there she is, watching me get ready to swim. She gives me a little wave and mouths 'I love you'. And its times like this that I know she is it.

She's the only one who could have saved me.

She's the only one I could ever want. The only one I could ever wish for.

She's mine.

Forever.

The End

Continue reading for a sneak peek at the next in the Into The Series, Into The Dark. Out now on Amazon.

Prologue

Mason

Just sitting here next to Rocco's hospital bed is killing me. I need to do something. Anything. I have been sitting listening to his steady breathing for six days now, well not his breathing, but the machine he's attached to, it makes a swishing noise every time it helps him breathe out. The first couple of days he was here I concentrated so hard on the machine, making sure it continued to work, convinced that if I slept it would stop and I would lose him forever. I just can't lose Rocco, he has been my best friend since we were both at school. I will never forget the first day he came to my school. We were both eight but unlike him I thought I was the shit. I laugh as I sit and think about it now. I went up to him like I was twice his age and told him that it was my playground, and he would follow my rules, or I would make everyone hate the new boy. His response wasn't exactly what I had expected, he punched me in the nose knocking me to the ground before he gave me a wedgie. He walked away from me saying, 'whatever' and I knew I needed to be friends with him. We have been inseparable ever since. Everywhere you found one of us, the other was never very far away. Starting our business together was like a dream come true, not even having to find a job would split us apart.

"You need to wake up now, Rocco. I need you here, there is no way I can do this all on my own." I lean forward and take his hand, praying that I feel it move even just the slightest amount, anything to prove that he will be ok. The doctors told me after the second operation on his spine that it was just a waiting game, he would wake up when his body decided it was healed. It's not enough for me, I need someone to tell me that he would wake up and be ok.

I hear the door of his room open, but I don't turn to see who it is, no one is more important at this moment than my best friend, the only brother I have ever known.

"Any change?" She says with such a dramatic sigh that I grab Rocco's hand tighter than I should, and I force myself to release some of the tension. I grind my teeth together to try and calm the anger that she always brings out in me.

"No. Everything is still the same, you would know if you stayed for more than five minutes at a time, Elle." I try to be nice. I really, really do, but I just can't manage it.

"Really, Mason? You may not have a life and can sit here all day every day, but I'm a busy person. My life can't stop because he's in here."

"Yeah, I can imagine your really busy. Oh, love the nails by the way." She goes slightly red as she realises that I know exactly what she gets up to while she isn't here, which is all the time.

"I thought you loved Rocco, you said he was your life. Now you can't even spend time with him when he needs you here." I can't even explain how much I hate Elle. Ever since Rocco had his accident she has had one excuse after another as to why she couldn't spend time at the hospital. From what I could tell the only reason she couldn't be here, is she is too busy out spending his money. It's like she is stockpiling everything she wants, just in case Rocco dies and his brother, Noah, gets everything. I close my eyes hoping that she will vanish into thin air. Even

191

looking at her makes the anger boil in my stomach, so I wish she would just leave and never come back.

"How dare you, Mason. I love Rocco. If he wakes up, I will give him all the support he needs. It's not like he knows we are even here, is it? So it's such a waste of time."

"When." I simply state.

"What do you mean? When? "

"You said if he wakes up. It's when he wakes up, Elle." I turn to look at her, giving her the full force of the anger I have inside. I swear that it's like she doesn't want him to wake up.

"Just go, Elle. You're no use to anyone here, you never were." Her back straightens and she glares at me, but I don't care.

"Will you call if there's any change?" She asks in clipped tone.

"Yeah, sure I will. You will be the first to know." I can't help the sarcasm that slips into my words, but she will be the last person who I call, I will call Rocco's postman before I call her. I hear her heels clicking on the tiled floor as she stomps towards the door, and a second later the door slams behind her. I let out a heavy breath. I have always hated Elle, she wasn't good enough for Rocco before the accident, but I hate her even more now. She was just proving the fact that I thought she was a heartless bitch.

"Rocco, I love you man but I swear if you don't dump her arse I'm not gonna be happy. So you need to wake up, so you can make me smile when I see you kick her to the kerb." I sit back in my chair and assume the position that I discovered won't completely kill my back. I cross my arms and straighten my legs out in front of me, trying to put no pressure on my back. These seats aren't the easiest to sleep in, but I'm so tired, and I let the gentle swish of the ventilator lull me to sleep. My last thought before I fell asleep was the same as it had been since the accident, 'it's time to wake up Rocco, I miss you.'

Acknowledgements

Sarah Elizabeth: You were there when I was crying and ready to throw the whole story in the bin. You have been my support since day one of my project. And even though you had so much on your own plate but you were always there for me, on the computer or on the phone. I love you lady more than you will ever know. Here is to finally to meeting this year and being able to fan girl together. But for your support and love you will always be one of my best friends.

Megan Noelle: You introduced me to this whole "book" world and even though there are some days that I could kick your butt for it, I love being here. You were one of the ones who told me I needed to tell my story and pestered me until I started! So you know if this book stinks, I totally blame you! I want to thank you for letting me rant at you even though you knew nothing about what I was going on about, and for letting me bitch and just laugh with me. You are a part of my life without even trying. I love you my American friend!

Claire Louise Harker: For being there to read about Rocco even when it was a poor imitation of what the book is now. You looked past the typos and saw the story I was trying to tell. For giving your time and feedback I thank you more than I ever can say.

Carrie Statdler: You lady need a big thank you. You took the slack in the blogging world when I had to disappear for days. You have been on my cheering squad telling everyone who would listen about this book. Thank you, thank you, thank you!

To my betas who have read sections of this and given me their honest feedback...thank you! Jane, Claire, Faye and Grace!

To all the blogs who helped me get my name out there, however little the share was, to help me when you knew nothing about my work meant so much!

Books, Coffee and Wine, A Book Whore's Obsession, Reading by the Book, Just One More Page, The Chronic Romantic, Garside's Book Bets, Read That, Hooked on Books, promiscuous book blog, Babu's Bookshelf, One More Chapter, Romance Addiction, Author Stalkers, The Whispering Pages Book Blog, Come To The Darkside We Have Books, Blushing Divas Book Reviews, Total Book Geek, Author Groupies, Angie's Reading Dungeon, Panty Dropping Book Blog, Four Brits And A Book, Erotica Book Club, Kelly's kindle Konfessions...and so many many more!

For all the authors who pimped out my stuff without reading a word I had written! You all rock and I love you all.

K. Langston, S.K Hartley, Megan Noelle, Sarah Elizabeth, Britni Hill, Courtney Cross and Writer Jude Ouvrard.

And to everyone who has taken time to read this book, I thank you! You have made a first time author very happy. I hope you love the story and I hope you love Rocco as much as I do.

Other information

The Into The series:

Into the Deep ~ Rocco and Makenzie's story is available now

Into the Dark ~ Mason and Niamh's story is available now

Into The Fire ~ Noah and Madison's story out now

Standalone Novels:

Leaving His Mark ~ Coming Spring 2015

Leaving Her Mark ~ Coming Summer 2015

Trying To Find Home ~ Coming Autumn 2015

Falling For Joe ~ Early 2016

Keep up to date with all my news:

Facebook: https://www.facebook.com/pages/Ta-Mckay-Author/1462902633937350

Twitter: https://twitter.com/tamckayauthor

Amazon author page: http://www.amazon.com/T.a.-McKay/e/B00JFF1R80/ref=sr_ntt_srch_lnk_1?qid=1411487268&sr=8-1

Goodreads:
https://www.goodreads.com/author/show/7750967.T_A_McKay

40550100R00113

Made in the USA
Charleston, SC
09 April 2015